A
SIMPLY WONDERFUL
CHRISTMAS

A Literary Advent Calendar

Illustrated by Silke Leffler

NORTHSOUTH
BOOKS
New York / London

For my Mamalia
S. L.

Contents

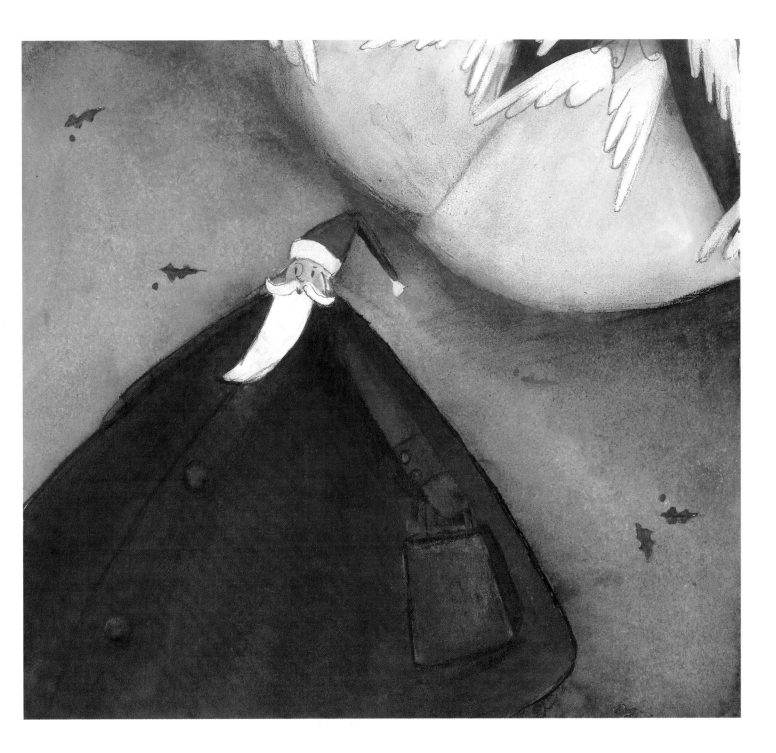

Hermann Mensing
CHRISTMAS ABC

ANGELS, WATCHING

BETTER NOT DISTURB

CANDLES, FLICKERING

DANCING SHADOWS, GET PREPARED

EVERY WISH

FULFILLED—MAYBE

GLIMPSES

HURRY SECRETLY

IS THERE . . . ?

JOY, THERE IS, INDEED

KEEP THE SECRET

LOVE IS ALL YOU NEED

MAKE IT SIMPLE

NEARER TO NOEL

OH, WHAT GOOD TIMES

PLEASE BE STILL

QUESTION NO MORE

RING THE JINGLE BELL

SING FOR SANTA, SENSE THE SWEETEST SMELL

TREES ARE DECORATED—WHAT DELIGHT

UAND I AND ALL SMILE BRIGHT

VISITORS ON CHRISTMAS EVE

WISHES FOR HEAVENLY PEACE

X FOR X-MAS **Y** FOR YULE, AND

ZED

DANCING, SINGING, NEVER GO TO BED . . .

Ulla Klomp

A NICHOLAS BY ANY OTHER NAME

"If only December were already over!" Nick sighed as he glanced at the Advent calendar that hung at the foot of his bed. Alas, the dreadful month of December had just begun.

For eleven months of the year, from January through November, Nick was a perfectly happy boy. But in December everything changed. For Nick, December was a month-long nightmare. And it was all because of his name, the official one written on his birth certificate: Nicholas Snow.

Sometimes it even started in mid-November. Everywhere he looked there were a thousand and one Saint Nicks, from pocket sized to life sized. They were stuffed, painted, baked, and even electric. They were made of wood, plastic, paper, and gingerbread. There were even Saint Nicholas tattoos. Nick was sick of all the Nicholases! Sometimes, he simply looked the other way. That improved his mood for a little while. But his bad mood quickly returned, when he heard the Christmas music playing in the stores. "Jolly Old Saint Nicholas," "Frosty the Snowman," and "Here Comes Santa Claus" rang out everywhere.

Nick Snow thought himself most worthy of pity. And if all those Saint Nicholases weren't bad enough, he had to put up with all the silly things people said to him throughout the entire Christmas season. "Better be careful, Snow, don't get so close to the heater or you'll melt!" or the ever-hilarious "When are you going to grow a long white beard?"

For Christmas, Nick Snow had often wished for a new name. Once, he suggested the name Matthew Andrews. He had found it in the phone book. Another time, he wanted to be called Adrian Sommers. That made him think of summer vacation and had nothing at all to do with Christmas.

Dad had said, "A new name? How ridiculous. Don't even think about it. Your grandfather was named Nicholas Snow."

At last, Nick decided that instead of going to school, he was going to go change his name. He rode the bus to City Hall.

Lots of people walked back and forth in the enormous entryway. Some had files tucked under their arms, some didn't. Many clutched a cell phone to their ear. The right-handed people had it at their right ear, the left-handed ones at the left. It

was almost as if they had cell phones growing there.

Nick went to the information desk. "Hello," he said, "I'm looking for the department where I can go to change my name."

"Change your name? Do you mean your last name?" asked the thin woman behind the counter. She looked a bit chilly.

"No, not just the last name. The first name, too," replied Nick.

The woman stared at him. "What? Both names? First name and last name? Do you know how much that costs?"

Why did adults always have to ask so many questions? thought Nick. "My name is Nicholas Snow," he said tersely. Thinking that this would explain everything.

The woman looked at him. Her eyes went from Nick to the life-sized, stuffed Santa Claus that stood in the foyer next to the nine-foot-tall fir tree.

"*Nicholas Snow?* Really?" The corners of her mouth twitched. Then she coughed. "That is a cute name. If I were you, I'd keep it."

"But I want another name," said Nick quietly. The woman blew her nose long and loud.

"You need to go to the County Clerk's office, young man. That's where they change names. First and last names!"

When Nick knocked at the door, a soft "Come in!" hailed from inside. Nick opened the door to Room 475 on the fourth floor and stepped into a large room, bathed in fluorescent light. There were many desks. Red Advent candles burned on two of them, and a small Saint Nicholas dressed in felt decorated the computer monitor of another. With lightning speed, Nick took a mental inventory of everything Christmasy—it was a habit he had.

"Hello, I would like to change my name," he announced. He figured he might as well get right to the point.

"You would like to change your name? Why? How old are you? Do your parents know that you are here? Besides, you know, it's not that easy to just change your name!" The blonde woman stared at Nick from behind the main counter.

Nick was starting to get upset. Again he was being bombarded with questions!

"What is your name, anyway?" she asked.

Another question. But he had to answer this one if he was going to get anywhere.

"Nicholas Snow. My name is Nicholas Snow."

"*Nicholas Snow?*"

Nick could almost see the laughter dancing through the woman's head. It didn't matter. He was determined to see this through. It had to happen this year. That's why he remained polite. His parents always told him to be polite to grown-ups.

"Yes, my name is Nicholas, Nicholas Snow. My name is, um … too Christmasy. It's as if the whole year were Christmas. I just can't stand it anymore," said Nick. "Especially not in December."

The woman laughed. First it was a hiccup, then a giggle that became louder and louder till it ended in loud peals of laughter.

"Nicholas Snow. That's very festive! Just like having Christmas all year long! Wait a minute, I have to tell my colleague about this!" She reached for the phone, lifted the receiver, and pressed a button. "Père, come quick. Yes, right away. There's a young man here with a terrific name. You have to meet him. His name is Nicholas Snow. And he wants to change it—can you believe it?"

She hung up and said, "Nicholas, guess what my name is?"

Nick shifted from one foot to the other. He would have preferred to leave. But that would have been giving up.

"Monster!" she said.

Nick looked around. Had a monster come through the door behind him? Or was the woman referring to him?

The woman looked at him and laughed heartily once again. "No, there's no monster behind you. That's my name! Mrs. Monster! Mrs. Beatrice Alice Monster—yes, my name is *B. A. Monster*! Now, isn't that a beastly name?"

Nick didn't know what to say. Just then, a young man entered and made a beeline for him. The man laughed. "So, you're Nicholas Snow? Then, we belong together. My name is Père, Père Noël, you know, Father Christmas! Have you gotten the sleigh out of the garage yet? We have to hurry. Nicholas Day is only four days away!"

Nick couldn't understand these two—they seemed happy about their names.

"Hey, Nicholas," said Mrs. Monster, "names are precious. They are the first gift you receive when you are born. They tell you that you are not alone, that you belong to a family, whether the family is called Scrap, or Monster, or Snow, or Nöel. And I'm sure that the Snow family is a nice family, one that you can be proud of.

The Monster family is monstrously nice, for example. And if anyone disagrees, they'll have to take it up with me!"

Later that evening, Nick was in bed again and glanced in the direction of the Advent calendar, just as he had that morning. That paper thing with the twenty-four doors was really old fashioned in this age of countless interactive Advent calendars on the World Wide Web. What was a name anyway, he thought. Even if there were a thousand and one Nicholases in the world it was still possible to be proud of the name Nicholas Snow. If Mrs. Monster and Père Noël could live with their names, then he could certainly live with his. And that's the feeling that Nicholas has embraced to this very day.

Renate Welsh

BABY JESUS TAKES A BATH

When I was a child my standard question from morning till night was: "Really? But why?" This caused any number of problems. First of all, no matter how much I contorted my tongue and my mouth, *R* was a sound I just could not pronounce. Again and again, really became *weally.* Of course no one took my question seriously. Everyone laughed, and laughed in a way that made me angry. On top of that, I, like all clever children, asked precisely those questions for which the grown-ups had no answers or ones that they found embarrassing.

"You wouldn't understand, you're still too young," they said, or else, "I'm sorry, I'm busy right now." Sometimes they went so far as to say, "Clean up your room first, it's such a mess." So, like all clever children, I also learned that sometimes it is up to you to figure out answers to the most important questions. In the meantime, I've gotten older and I know that behind every question lurks another question, that behind every mountain there is another mountain, and that answers are rare and are often almost too small to see.

Looking at a picture book one day, I was faced with a problem. Why did the Christ Child have golden ringlets like a girl, when the painting in church clearly showed that Baby Jesus was a boy? Obviously, the adult Jesus was a man.

"Is the Christ Child Baby Jesus' sister?" I asked my grandmother, and then the mailman and other important people. Of course I did not get an answer, only smiles.

"The ideas this child has!" my grandmother remarked to my father. I didn't ask him. If the others smiled, he would surely laugh at me. I hated it when he did that.

We had a manger with a little wax Jesus—a gift from the nuns at Saint Joseph's where Dad was a doctor. Baby Jesus had become a bit dusty over the years and was positively gray between his fingers and toes. I decided he needed a bath, so I lifted him carefully out of the straw and laid him on my bed while I dusted the manger thoroughly and cleaned out all the nooks and crannies. I picked up each individual piece of straw and blew on it before replacing it in the manger. I washed the little muslin square that had

"Now I lay me down to sleep..."

served as a sheet with a brush and soap and pressed it smoothly against the edge of the bath.

I filled the basin with water, tested it with my elbow to see that it was warm, but not too hot, and then fetched Baby Jesus. His diaper wouldn't come off. It had been glued to his little bottom! I held his curly haired head with one hand and carefully washed his small hands and feet with my other hand.

Suddenly I felt a movement in my left hand, as if a finger had gently tapped my palm. I cried out, but no one heard me. My heart beat wildly, and my knees trembled.

"Now I lay me down to sleep," I whispered. It was the only prayer I could think of. I was so flustered I couldn't remember the rest. "Now I lay me down to sleep."

There it was again. That movement. I almost dropped Baby Jesus. I picked him up out of the water and laid him on a towel. I felt sick and the bathroom seemed to be spinning.

"Now I lay me down to sleep; I pray the Lord my soul to keep. If I should die before I wake, I pray the Lord my soul to take." The prayer had come back to me and I could breathe again. When I opened my eyes, the bathtub was standing still, as it should. So was the basin and the cabinet.

Baby Jesus lay there on the white towel, as waxy as before, the left leg bent and the right one stretched out, as though ready to kick, but where there had been five delicate toes, there was now a misshapen lump! Our Baby Jesus now had a clubfoot.

It took me a long time before I realized that the wax had gone soft in the warm water. "I didn't mean to do that, I really didn't! I just wanted to make you look nice and clean for Christmas," I said. "Don't be angry. Please don't be angry."

Baby Jesus' smile was as sweet as before. Now I was terrified about what my parents would say. I didn't dare dry Jesus for fear that something else might happen. So I blew on him gently, trying to dry him. Meanwhile, the little sheet had dried on the edge of the bathtub. I spread it on the straw and laid Baby Jesus down. "See how nice the manger looks now," I whispered.

But all I could see was the lump where Baby Jesus' tiny foot had once been. The clubfoot accused me. I was sure that everyone would see it.

I scattered some straw over it, hoping that no one would notice. Then I carried the manger into the dining room and put it back on the sideboard.

Baby Jesus still smiled. As I turned away, I saw him wink. He really did! And the proof is that no one ever noticed the clubfoot. Not even my grandmother, and she always saw everything!

Barbara Veit
BARBARA'S BLOSSOMS

When Barbara woke up on December 4, it was a day like any other. Dad had already left for work. Mom told her to hurry—she was late again! Then, with a hug and a kiss, Mom was off to her job.

Barbara tucked her lunch into her schoolbag, put her jacket on and then slowly took it off again, and sat back down at the breakfast table. She was tired. She had spent too much time reading under the covers last night with a flashlight. She just wanted to sit for five more minutes, eat a banana, and think about the book she had been reading.

The phone rang just as she was taking her last bite of banana.

"Mmmpf," she answered, then, "hello!"

"What does 'mmmpf, hello' mean?" asked a deep voice.

"Th-th-that means . . . I'm sorry, this is Barbara!" Barbara mumbled, embarrassed.

"Th-th-that sounds better already," replied the deep voice. "This is Saint Nicholas, wishing you a happy Name Day!"

"Wh-wh-what?" stammered Barbara.

"Since when do you stutter?" laughed a familiar voice.

"Gosh, Grandpa!" Barbara sighed, relieved. "You really fooled me!"

"Did I manage to do that again?" Her grandfather giggled happily. "Best wishes, my dear! What did you get for Name Day?"

Barbara didn't answer. Neither Mom nor Dad had remembered her Name Day. She hadn't even remembered it herself. The same thing happened last year, too, she recalled.

"Ooops," she mumbled, "I don't think we celebrate that."

"Oh!" said her grandfather. "We'll change that today! I hereby declare today a school holiday and invite you to come over to spend it with

me! If you hurry, you can be here in half an hour! See you soon!"

She heard a click as her grandfather hung up. Barbara stood in the hallway, perplexed. Surely she couldn't just skip school. Grandpa probably just wanted to annoy her parents again. He liked to do that. He believed that people worked too much in today's society, and only did it so they could buy themselves silly things they didn't need. Barbara had to laugh as she thought of the funny arguments Grandpa had with Mom. Grandpa didn't take the arguments seriously, but Mom would hit the roof.

Barbara loved Grandpa, and that's why it

didn't take her long to make up her mind. She dropped her schoolbag, bolted out of the house, grabbed her bicycle, and rode over to his house.

It was a mild morning, much too warm for December. It had rained overnight, but now the sun was shining and the wet leaves smelled good. Grandpa was waiting in front of his small house carrying his old sheepskin jacket, which Mom kept trying to get him to throw away.

"Come on!" he called. "Put your bike away. Let's take a walk through the garden." Typical Grandpa. A walk through the garden! For this, she had risked getting into all kinds of trouble with her parents and at school. Grandpa was already plodding toward the orchard without waiting for her. Barbara leaned her bicycle against the shed and ran behind him.

"Pick out the nicest twigs with the fullest buds and I will cut them for you," said Grandpa when she caught up with him.

"Wh . . . why?" asked Barbara.

"You are stuttering again!" Grandpa grinned.

"I will tell you why we are cutting twigs—because today is Saint Barbara's Day!"

Barbara stood still and looked at Grandfather skeptically. Was this another one of his jokes? But Grandfather looked more serious than usual as he leaned against an apple tree and said, "You know, people forget all of the little things that are important in life. Each name has a meaning, otherwise we would all be called 'refrigerator' or 'oven'!"

Barbara had to laugh. She had never thought about this. She found some names pretty, others boring or silly. But the idea that they had meaning had not occurred to her.

"What does Barbara mean?" asked Barbara, holding her breath for a moment.

"In Latin, it means the stranger or the barbarian. That's fitting for you, isn't it?"

Barbara grimaced. "Nothing else?" she asked.

"Yes," her grandfather answered. "It was also the name of a strong young woman who has long been honored as a saint. She lived 1,700 years ago in Nicomedia, a city in what is now Turkey. She is said to have been very beautiful and wise, this Barbara. She was also Christian, which was dangerous, because Turkey belonged to the Roman Empire and the Romans persecuted all Christians. Barbara's father was a wealthy merchant. He had absolutely no understanding of her faith in Christ.

He thought she should

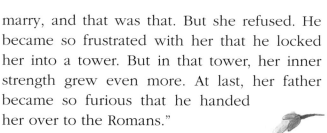

marry, and that was that. But she refused. He became so frustrated with her that he locked her into a tower. But in that tower, her inner strength grew even more. At last, her father became so furious that he handed her over to the Romans."

"What? Her own father?" Barbara looked at her grandfather in disbelief.

"Yes, her own father! Some fathers become very cross when their daughters don't do as they are told!"

"And what did the Romans do with her?"

"Well, they demanded that she renounce her faith. Which, of course, she didn't."

"And then?"

Grandpa furrowed his brow and scratched his head a bit uncomfortably. "She was sentenced to death and died very bravely. Soon thereafter, the legend says, her father was struck by lightning."

"Serves him right!" said Barbara.

"Yes, I think so, too!" said Grandpa. "Now you know that your patron saint was a very brave woman. Among Christians, she is known as a protector of

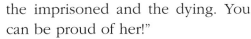

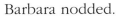

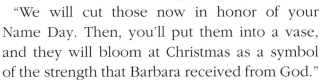

the imprisoned and the dying. You can be proud of her!"

Barbara nodded.

"And what about the twigs?"

"We will cut those now in honor of your Name Day. Then, you'll put them into a vase, and they will bloom at Christmas as a symbol of the strength that Barbara received from God."

They cut a bouquet of apple and cherry twigs in silence. Later, they drank hot chocolate and had a long conversation about Barbara's name and many other names. It was the nicest day Barbara had ever spent with Grandpa. Before she left his house, he wrote her an excuse for missing school. Barbara placed her twigs into a vase and checked them carefully every day. And then, just before Christmas, the first ones bloomed, delicate white flowers in the midst of winter, reminding her of her namesake and the love of her grandfather.

MEMORY PAGES

Here is a place for your own holiday memories, recipes, traditions, photos, and more!

MEMORY PAGES

MEMORY PAGES

MEMORY PAGES

MEMORY PAGES

Sigrid Laube
KIDNAPPING SAINT NICK

"Paul," called Anna. Then louder, "Paul, why aren't you answering?"

It was dark outside. Cold fog had turned into frost, which now coated the garden's branches in white. It was December 4, and Christmas seemed impossibly far away. Paul was immersed in his French textbook. The test was in three days, and he had failed the last one.

A branch tapped against the windowpane like a skeleton's warning finger. Paul was startled.

"Quiet!" he growled, angrily. "If I had known how hard it would be, I would have picked a different language."

"Si j'avais su . . ." translated his twin sister, Anna. She had stepped quietly into Paul's room, and then let the door slam shut behind her.

"Show-off," Paul hissed. He leaned back in his chair with a sigh. "What are you doing here? French isn't your problem." It was true. Anna was a good student, and French grammar did not faze her.

"Keep failing and French won't be your main problem, either, Mom and Dad will be," answered Anna as she sat down.

"Tell me about it," fumed Paul. "What's up?"

"Well, for one thing, Grandpa is in the hospital with a broken leg."

"And?" Paul retorted. He quickly corrected himself, "Poor Grandpa! I'll go visit him tomorrow."

"But that's not going to help him the day after tomorrow," said Anna.

"The day after tomorrow? What are you talking about?" asked Paul, confused.

"Okay. The day after tomorrow is Saint Nicholas Day. And that's when Grandpa always comes over in the evening with his red robe, big bushy beard, chocolate, and embarrassing questions about how we have behaved."

"Well, not this year," mused Paul, thinking that this was actually a shame.

"And you're fine with that?" his sister continued.

"No, of course not." Paul hesitated, and thought some more. Then, he scratched his head and added, crestfallen, "I can't very well bring him his bushy beard at the hospital and stand there confessing my sins, can I?"

"No," said Anna, "but don't you think that he's going to miss his Nicholas performance?"

30

"Sure," nodded Paul. Grandpa resembled Nicholas all year round. He had sparkling blue eyes, snow-white hair, and liked to wear boots with his jeans. He was a cool Nicholas, really. And, as long as Anna and her brother could remember, he had come every December 6, just as dusk fell. He appeared dressed in his red bathrobe and a fluffy cotton beard that he crafted new each year. The twins had always known that it was their grandfather, reciting Christmas poetry in his deep voice. Paul would always claim, "You're not the real Saint Nicholas."

"That doesn't matter," the would-be Saint Nicholas would reply. "Have you been good children?"

He asked about their sins and then gave them fruit and sweets. It had always been a welcome treat before Christmas. The red bathrobe had survived many performances, with its threadbare sleeves and worn collar. But now Grandpa lay in the hospital with a broken leg. Paul sighed.

"What can we do?" he asked. His French grammar exercises were forgotten.

Anna thought about it. Then she hit him on the shoulder.

"I have it!" she cried. "If Saint Nicholas can't come to the mountain, then . . ."

". . . the mountain must come to Saint Nicholas," Paul completed.

"Yes! We will visit Grandpa," said Anna.

"Huh? How is that a solution?" objected Paul.

"It's a solution because we will bring Saint Nicholas to visit him this time! And we will bring him chocolate and ask embarrassing questions. Don't you think that will please him?"

"To visit him as Saint Nicholas? How is that supposed to work? You are a girl and I don't have a deep voice." It bothered Paul that he was the last boy in his class who still had a high voice.

"Well, then, we'll find a Nicholas to go with us," answered Anna.

"And where will we find a Nicholas, smarty-pants? Do you think we can just grab one standing around on the street?" Paul was getting annoyed. Anna always thought everything was so easy.

"I'll think of something," said Anna with resolve as she stood up. "Keep studying your French grammar, and I will take care of the rest. It will be a surprise—Grandpa will be so thrilled." She left the room, excited.

The moste beautiful gifts come from Sommers Department Store

"I hope that goes well," mumbled Paul. His glance fell to the next exercise. "Drat!"

The next evening, Paul asked his twin, "So, did you find a Nicholas?"

"No," was her downcast response. "All of the boys in the class are busy studying French. Dad is on a business trip tomorrow, and Uncle William, who has such a nice voice, is in bed with a cold."

"What do we do now?" Paul was nervous.

"Time will tell." Anna was in a hurry. She was meeting several friends at the movie theater, and that was all she could think of right now.

December 6 was sunny and cloudless. The twins were eating breakfast.

"Did you find a Nicholas last night?" Paul asked with his mouth full.

Anna stared into her bowl and began to dig furrows into her oatmeal.

"No," she said dejectedly.

"You probably had other things to do," sneered her brother. It made him angry that something so simple as finding a replacement Nicholas seemed so impossible to accomplish.

"If I had known that," he added furiously, "I would have taken care of it myself. Now it is a little late, don't you think? There are only nine hours until the afternoon, and I have to spend six of those in school. As do you, for that matter."

"Oh, don't be such a nag," said Anna. But she was disappointed as well. The night at the movies had been fun. But she had completely forgotten about solving the Nicholas problem.

"Fine, I'll go look for a Nicholas. How hard can it be?" Paul finished his tea and slammed his cup down onto the table.

"Whatever," answered Anna snippily. Then they took separate paths to school.

The morning dragged on. Paul brooded during his lessons. The problem had to have a solution! They couldn't disappoint Grandpa. His grandchildren owed him a little bit of Nicholas joy. But when the afternoon bell rang and the class left school noisily, Paul shuffled dejectedly behind. Where on Earth could one find a spare Nicholas?

The streets were decorated in Christmas finery. Strings of lights hung from the trees, colorful balls with tinsel and glittering arrangements competed in display windows to grab shoppers' attention. Paul moped along with downcast eyes. The sun had set behind the buildings' high rooftops and a cold, shallow light spread through the city.

"I don't have much time left," Paul muttered to himself. "Poor Grandpa."

Then he heard a quiet ringing.

It was a tinkling sound, like a little bell. The wind picked it up, blowing the silvery tones through the alley. Paul looked up. An oncoming car blinded him and an old man bumped into him. "Watch where you're going, kid!"

Paul apologized automatically. He heard the bell again. It came closer. No, not just the bell came closer, but an entire Santa Claus, a magnificent Santa Claus, complete with ringing bell. Tall and broad-shouldered, he rang the bell with one hand while holding a sign in the other. In elaborate golden script, the sign read: "The most beautiful gifts come from Sommer's Department Store." He strolled leisurely down the street.

Suddenly Paul had an idea. He rushed to the Santa, almost falling into his arms. "Hey, take it easy," said the Santa in a very un-Santa-like manner. Stopping, he cleared his throat, "Ahem, I mean, what do you want for Christmas, my boy? Have you been behaving yourself?"

"Yes," Paul answered quickly, "but there's not time for that. Right now, I need your help."

"Now, now, my son," the Santa began with a deep voice.

"P-p-please, let me explain," Paul stammered and stood before the Santa, blocking his path. The Santa looked down at the boy. Then, he leaned his sign against a house and stroked his beard.

"Tell me what is wrong," he said. "But hurry up. Can't you see that I am a little busy?"

But he didn't sound angry or impatient.

"Tell me this, are you supposed to be a Santa Claus?" asked Paul, confused.

"Are you blind, my boy?" The Santa laughed out loud. "What else would I be?"

"Could you perhaps be a Nicholas as well? I mean, if needed, and if I asked you nicely?" The whole crazy story about his injured grandpa, the French test, and the urgency of visiting Grandpa in the hospital tumbled out. He ended his explanation hesitantly, "I was wondering if I could, uh, sort of kidnap you for a little while. It's for a good cause."

The Santa listened quietly, occasionally nodding thoughtfully. He glanced at the date displayed on his fancy sport watch and said, "Let me see, my boy. Well, it really is December 6 today. So why not play Nicholas for a change? Santa Claus must be flexible after all. Lead the way. You can kidnap me, and I will come with you to visit your grandpa. Where is the hospital?" Paul leaped into the air. Then he asked, almost reverently, "Are people allowed to give Santa Claus a hug?"

"Better not," the Santa replied. "Otherwise, my beard might fall off. And that would be undignified, you understand."

Paul nodded. He suddenly became serious. "What will we do about my sister, Anna?" he asked. She is probably sitting at home, racking her brains trying to find a Nicholas." He looked around. Twilight had come, and the first star shone in the sky.

"It is already late, and visiting hours end at 4:30." He shook his head, sadly. "Oh, forget it, Mr. Santa Claus. It was a good idea, but it won't work."

"Come, come—don't give up so quickly. You don't know Nicholas very well. And don't you believe in Santa?" The stranger tucked his sign under his arm and stuffed the bell into one pocket while he pulled a cell phone out of another.

"Even Santa has to keep up with the latest technology. What is your sister's phone number and how far is it to the hospital?"

It almost took Paul's breath away. He cheered up, quickly dictated the number, and provided the directions.

"We'll make it," Paul heard him mumble. "We still have an hour." He calmly told Anna what she had to do. "Don't forget the cookies and bring some chocolate, too," he said. "And you'd better bring some fruit. Sick people need vitamins—oranges, apples, and all that. Do you have a backpack? Good, bring that so I have something to pull the goodies out of." Satisfied, he tucked the phone back into his pocket. "We better hurry, we're meeting your sister at the main entrance. Oh, yes, one more thing, has your grandpa behaved himself? How did he break his leg? I'll have to ask him a few embarrassing questions, after all."

Rushing up the hospital steps, they ran right into the heavily laden Anna, who was coming from the other direction. "Thank you, dear Nicholas, whoever you are," she began breathlessly.

"No thanks, please," he said. "Duty is duty. Now, let's get to work." He tucked his "The most beautiful gifts come from Sommer's Department Store" sign behind a column.

He straightened his beard and hat, adjusted his locks, and tightened his belt. Anna gave him the backpack. Apparently, she had raided Mom's fruit basket thoroughly. It felt like it weighed a ton. The clock over the entrance struck slowly four times. It was almost dark. Together, they went into the hospital ward.

The nurses looked surprised as they saw the group enter. One smiled and said, "Isn't that a cute idea."

Nicholas winked cheerfully and greeted everyone with a nod. His shoes squeaked on the linoleum and his cloak flowed around him.

"Here, this is Grandpa's room," Paul whispered.

"Go ahead and knock, my boy. Loudly," said Nicholas.

Paul knocked and then opened the door. He fought a lump in his throat. Grandpa lay back on his pillows. He looked very small and frail.

In a loud voice, Nicholas began the familiar Christmas poem. Grandpa smiled.

Outside the moon was rising.

Jutta Treiber
CHRISTMAS MARKET

The Christmas market in the town square looked beautiful. There was a large Christmas tree and a manger with life-sized figures. Real sheep and goats roamed around the nativity scene. My mother was thrilled. My father was more interested in the booths selling food and beverages.

First, I followed my father to the food section. The men there were busy talking about absolutely nothing interesting, so I went to have a look at the kids' nativity area and watched the sheep. A Christ Child with a silver dress and golden hair danced around. A brass band played at the other side of the square. A choir sang Christmas songs.

My mother was anxiously looking in the craft booths. It was only 4 o'clock in the afternoon, but it was already dark, and she couldn't seem to find any Christmas presents. She was annoyed that Dad wasn't helping her with the gift buying.

Suddenly, I spotted a booth that looked a little different. My mother had stopped, too. Fascinated, she pointed at a little nativity scene. "Look," she said, "isn't it beautiful?"

There was a wooden stable with a star above it. The figures, Mary, Joseph, the manger, the ox, and the donkey, were all made of clay. A shepherd, who appeared to be herding a few sheep, stood outside the stable. On the right there was a figure that was probably supposed to be an angel. It was very unusual. He had a large face and was earthy brown. He looked a little like our neighbor who had Down syndrome. And then I noticed that this booth belonged to a workshop for people with disabilities.

The disabled workers had made the nativity themselves—the wooden stable as well as the clay figures. I thought this was the most beautiful nativity in the whole Christmas market. It was much nicer than the factory-made ones.

Of course, my mother had to buy it.

The workers wrapped each figure in tissue paper and laid them carefully in a box. Mom dragged Dad away from his friends and made him carry the stable.

Once we got back home, Mom unwrapped the nativity. "I'll set it up on the sideboard right away," she said. "Maybe that will give us all a little Christmas spirit." I braced myself for a lengthy complaint about Dad's lack of Christmas spirit and the stress of the season.

Mom cleaned off the sideboard and placed the wooden stable on it. Then we carefully unpacked the figures and set them inside: Mary, Joseph, the manger, the ox, the donkey, and the angel with Down syndrome. Mom was delighted. Dad had fallen asleep on the living room couch.

Suddenly, my mom froze. "The child is missing!" she shouted.

"I'm right here!" I said.

"Don't be silly, Frank!" Mom said. "I meant the child in the manger. It's missing!" Sure enough—the manger was empty.

I could have predicted word for word the list of complaints that would come now. The worker hadn't packed the child. He had dropped it next to the box. He had stepped on it. It had fallen out of the box on the way home (although this possibility was highly unlikely). It had fallen on the floor as we were unpacking. And, of course, it was all Dad's fault because poor Mom had to do everything.

We began searching the floor. I crawled under the table. I found cake crumbs, a marble, and a safety pin, but no Christ Child. I looked behind the sideboard. I found a smelly, old sock, but no Christ Child. Mom was ready to get dressed and retrace the entire way back to the Christmas market to look for the child.

"It's dark," said my father from the couch. "You wouldn't find it even if it were life sized."

I stood before the sideboard and peered into the manger. I could not remember what the child had looked like. "Perhaps there was no Christ Child," I said.

"Nonsense!" said Mother. "There is no such thing as a manger without a Christ Child." Somehow, she was right.

Dad had reluctantly joined the search. I examined the figures more closely: Joseph dressed in brown, the empty manger, the ox lying down, the donkey standing upright, the sheep with its curly, white wool, the shepherd in a wide, green cloak, the angel with Down syndrome, and gentle Mary, dressed in blue.

And then I saw it—tiny, barely noticeable, and extremely snug.

"There it is," I said. "The child. There, don't you see? Mary has taken it into her arms."

In that one silent moment, it seemed that all the stress, arguments, and worries of the season had fallen away.

The three of us stood in wonder and, just like the family in the stable, we gazed at that small, perfect child nestled in his mother's arms. Never in my life had I seen such a nativity.

Kerstin Dresing

RUDOLPH AND BRITTA

Sandy could hear her brother singing as he came up the stairs.

"Rudolph, the red-nosed reindeer . . ."

She groaned. "Here comes Rudolph!" she called to her mother, who was in the kitchen.

Rudolph's name was actually Jacob. He was Sandy's younger brother, and he was crazy about reindeer. He was in the first grade, where he'd recently learned that irritating song "Rudolph, the Red-Nosed Reindeer." To make it all worse, last year Grandma had given him a Rudolph toy, which he played with year round!

". . . had a very shiny nose . . ." Jacob threw open the door, continuing to belt out his song as he took off his coat, ". . . and if you ever saw it . . ."

Sandy covered her ears. The endless singing was driving her crazy.

"Mooommm!" she cried for help. Mom just stood laughing at the kitchen door and dried her hands.

Judging by the loudness of the singing, he was headed straight for her room.

As the door opened, a pillow sailed by Jacob's head, along with the sharp command, "Would you shush already?"

"Why?" said Jacob, kicking the pillow. "I sing much better than Britta Steer," Jacob shot back.

"Ugh! Her name is Britney Spears!"

Luckily, Mom stepped in just in time. "That's enough, you two. It's time to eat."

No sooner had they sat down than Jacob began to chatter. At least he's not singing, thought Sandy, gritting her teeth.

"This morning, I met Mrs. Seitz in the stairwell, and I saw her again this afternoon." Jacob never stopped talking.

"Fascinating," said Sandy sarcastically. She was not fond of old Mrs. Seitz. She lived on the ground floor, was older than dirt, and very fussy. If you didn't wipe your shoes properly, she complained. If you were too loud, she complained. Recently, when Sandy had left the building door open, she had yelled at her. All right, maybe she did have a point—it was winter, but a little fresh air never hurt anyone.

"Really?" Mom asked Jacob.

"I gave her my Rudolph."

"You what?" Sandy's shout came so suddenly that a tortellini flew out of her mouth and across the table.

"Eeeuww, gross, Sandy," said Jacob before continuing. "She came out to talk to me this morning. She said she likes my singing."

"I bet she'd like your silence even more," Sandy suggested helpfully.

"She would not. She thinks my singing is great. She likes my Rudolph, too."

"You gave it to her?" Sandy couldn't believe it.

"Actually, I only let her borrow it for a little while." Jacob shrugged his shoulders. "She thought he was so cute and she lives all by herself. She wants us to come by for fruitcake. She said I should bring my beautiful sister with me. I don't have any other sisters, do I, Mom?" He grinned.

What a little rat! "No way am I going," said Sandy defiantly.

"Come on," Mom patted her hand. "It's Christmastime. Think of it as a good deed. You don't have to stay long. She probably doesn't get many visitors and she'll be so happy to have you."

"No way," said Sandy with certainty. But the next day, she ended up going after all. Jacob had said Mrs. Seitz would think Sandy was a stuck-up pig if she didn't.

Mom sent along a small candle arrangement. Sandy was a little nervous as she stood in front of the door. She wasn't sure what she should say. After all, she'd recently been in trouble with Mrs. Seitz. Her brother hopped from one foot to the other, as excited as if they were visiting Santa Claus himself.

"Well, hello you two! What a nice surprise!" Mrs. Seitz beamed as she answered the door. "I just finished baking the fruitcake!"

Jacob gave Sandy a shove and pointed to her hand.

"Oh, right. Er, here you are. This is from Mom for you, for Christmas."

"It's from all of us," Jacob corrected. What a goody-goody. Sandy gave him a withering glance, which he didn't notice, as they were ushered in.

"Then I am especially pleased." Mrs. Seitz smiled at Sandy. "I thought you might be angry with me because I scolded you about the front door."

Jacob took a breath, but swallowed his comment when he saw Sandy's glance.

"Of course not," she said, blushing.

"Let's go into the kitchen," said their hostess. "By the way, Sandy, I am very sorry. I didn't mean to yell at you. I overreacted. But I'd been sick, and this building is so drafty in the winter. Will you forgive me? Your brother has told me a lot about you."

"No problem. I'm sorry I left the door open." Great, thought Sandy, I wonder what the little twerp has been telling her about me.

Jacob quickly ducked into the kitchen. It was warm, and the air smelled delicious.

"I will make some coffee for myself and some hot chocolate for you. Then we will have some fruitcake. I hope you'll like it!"

Smiling, she set Mom's candle right in the middle of the table.

Sandy and Jacob loved the fruitcake. The hot chocolate was better than any kind they'd ever tasted. Mrs. Seitz told stories about how she had celebrated Christmas as a child. Sandy forgot that she didn't want to be there and found herself laughing—a lot.

It was only when they lit the candles because it was getting dark that Sandy realized that they had been there for a long time. Mrs. Seitz finally said, "I think you'd better be getting home before your mother gets worried. I hope you will visit me again soon. I have a little something for you in case we don't see each other again before Christmas." She opened a closet and took out Jacob's Rudolph. "The doll doctor has freshened up your friend. He was pretty worn in some spots."

Turning to Sandy, she said, "I hope you like this. Jacob told me you are a big fan of Britta Steer." Mrs. Seitz giggled. Sandy started turning red, but then Mrs. Seitz said, "Jacob hummed one of the songs for me, and I realized he meant Britney Spears."

Sandy's mouth fell open. Mrs. Seitz smiled as she pressed the CD into Sandy's hand. "Can you imagine the looks they gave me at the music store when an old lady like me asked for the latest Britney Spears CD?"

Jacob raised his eyebrows and gave first Rudolph and then Mrs. Seitz a kiss on the nose.

After that afternoon, Sandy was always careful to close the building door all the way, and even to stop by for fruitcake and hot chocolate with her new friend every now and then.

Susanne Keller

TOO CLOSE FOR COMFORT

Unfortunately, the two street cleaners were almost exactly the same height. If it weren't for that, then the accident would never have happened.

Neither one was particularly tall. To be precise, one was just a teeny tiny bit smaller than the other, by about two inches. They wore bright orange uniforms and each carried a shovel on their shoulder.

If you should see two street cleaners of about the same size walking one behind the other, it almost seems like you are seeing double. At first you think it must be a trick of the eye—that surely there is only one street cleaner with a shovel on his shoulder. But there aren't too many people with double vision. And, if a person with double vision had walked down the street at that moment, glanced over, and seen double, he would have seen four similarly sized street cleaners. If someone sees double, he probably cannot tell from a distance whether one is two inches taller than the other, even if it looks like maybe four inches, since four is the double of two. This person with double vision *would* see a great deal of orange. Perhaps this person would then become hungry for an orange, or that is, for two.

Of course that is an advantage at Christmastime, when this story takes place, because those who do not eat oranges catch colds easily. Unless, of course, you live in Australia, where it is warm enough to have a picnic at the beach at Christmas. That is in contrast to where the accident involving the two similarly sized street cleaners took place. This presumably happened in a place where no one celebrates Christmas at the beach the way they might in Australia or Florida. Not only is it much too cold, it would never occur to anyone to have a Christmas picnic, because of all the snow.

Snow lay on the sidewalks, and it was up to the street cleaners to help remove it with their shovels. After all, that was their job. "Please shovel the snow," said their boss. Every street cleaner must listen to his boss, even a cleaner who is terribly allergic to snow.

Now the accident would not have happened if the street cleaner in front had been fifteen inches taller than the one behind him, instead of merely two. But, one has the height that one has, and that's that. Nothing can be done about that. The accident would also not have happened if a cat at the edge of the sidewalk had not stopped and looked up at the sky. It would be unfair to claim that it was the cat's

fault, since it really had nothing to do with the street cleaner's height. Anyway, the cat had paid no attention to the two men. On the contrary, she had looked longingly at the sky. Perhaps the cat was waiting for the Star of Bethlehem. After all, it was almost Christmas. Or maybe she was just waiting for birds.

The street cleaner in front, who was two inches taller, did not see the cat, perhaps because his thoughts were elsewhere. Perhaps they were where the street cleaners do not have to shovel snow at Christmas, or where no one has cold ears at Christmas. The rear street cleaner, however, did see the cat.

He thought she looked very cute, sitting there as she waited, maybe for the Star of Bethlehem. He found the sight so beautiful that he called to his colleague, "Would you look at that cat." And then it happened.

It seems ridiculous that an accident could occur simply because of one's size. But when the street cleaner in front turned around to look at the cat, his shovel swung round as well and *smack*! He slammed his shovel straight into his colleague's ear. A fine mess! The street cleaner in the back got three days without work, a constant ringing in his ears, and a reminder to always wear a hard hat in the future.

Monika Felten
PENG-YO

"Oh, come, little children, oh . . ." Phillip half-heartedly opened and closed his mouth, pretending to sing along. Of everything school-related, he hated music more than anything. Well, actually, he hated homework most of all.

He looked out the window without interrupting his silent singing. There was no snow on the ground, but it was freezing cold. Perfect weather for ice-skating! The lake had been approved for ice-skating yesterday. Phillip couldn't wait. In his head, he pictured himself skating over ice as smooth as glass. Unfortunately, he had to do his homework first—a ton of it. He sighed as the class continued to sing, "More lovely than angels, this Baby so mild . . ."

Embarrassed, Phillip looked around to see if anyone had noticed. But no one seemed to have heard him. Tai-Kin smiled at him, but Phillip wasn't sure why he was smiling. Just to be safe, he smiled back. Tai-Kin had recently moved here from China, and he hadn't made any friends yet. This was partially because the

popular kids in seventh grade had decided not to be friendly to Tai-Kin on his very first day.

Phillip observed Tai-Kin out of the corner of his eye. The boy wasn't singing along, either. That was probably because he didn't know the words. Last week, the teacher had explained that Christmas was not widely celebrated in China. No Christmas? How could that be?

Rrrring! The school bell tore Phillip from his daydream. At last! Ice-skating! But first, Phillip sighed—there was homework.

It was already dark by the time Phillip got to the lake. The ice was well lit by an array of floodlights rigged along the shore, but it was surprisingly empty. Phillip glanced across the ice. His friends, Sam and Steven, were already there. The evening was saved! Then he spotted the bullies from the seventh grade at the other end of the lake. This did not bode well. Maybe skating tonight wasn't such a good idea after all. Oh, what the heck! Phillip laced up his skates with determination and sped off. He wouldn't let a handful of bullies wreck his fun. After all, he wasn't alone. His friends were there, too.

All was well for a little while and the three friends glided around undisturbed—until the bullies became bored.

"Hey, runts," Phillip heard their leader, Marc, call out. He saw Marc rushing toward them. Runts, indeed! How obnoxious! Phillip was getting angry, but held his tongue. You just never knew with Marc.

But Steven, who was not afraid of anyone, retorted brashly, "Takes one to know one!" Phillip bit his lower lip. Here comes trouble, he thought as Marc came closer, stopping in front of Steven. "Say that again, shrimp."

"Takes one to know one," repeated Steven, grinning as he sped off like lightning. Marc followed in hot pursuit. Steven was an outstanding skater. Again and again, he turned around and made faces at Marc. Marc huffed along behind him, his face bright red with anger and exhaustion. "Just wait until I catch you," he yelled.

"Slowpoke!" Steven jeered. And that's when it happened. Steven tripped on something on the surface of the ice. Phillip held his breath in horror. He heard Marc cry out triumphantly, but that is not what scared him.

As if in slow motion, he saw Steven slide across the smooth ice, right toward the section that was closed off because of thin ice.

Sam and the bullies suddenly became very

quiet. Unable to move, they waited for the impending catastrophe. Only Phillip reacted.

"Steeeeven," he screamed as he rushed over. Phillip knew he wouldn't be able to stop him. Steven had already slid so far out onto the thin, fragile ice that he couldn't follow him.

"Careful, Phillip!" Phillip slid past the red-and-white tape that marked the danger zone. "I, uh, this wasn't what I had in mind," Marc stammered unhappily. But no one was paying any attention to Marc. All eyes were focused on Steven, who had finally come to a stop about five yards beyond the tape. The thin ice creaked and cracked threateningly. Phillip didn't care. Without thinking, he ducked under the tape, lay flat on his stomach, and crawled toward Steven. "Don't move, Steven," he warned as he inched closer and closer to his friend.

Steven nodded weakly, his face filled with terror. Only four more yards! By now, the ice around Phillip crackled with every move. A crack ripped through the ice, right in front of his nose. Phillip froze. The ice couldn't be more than two inches thick at this point. Crawling any farther would have been pure madness. Phillip raised his head and saw Steven reaching for him. A large puddle of water had already formed around his friend, as his weight pushed the ice downward.

Phillip gathered all of his courage and moved closer to Steven. His heart raced. A quick glance over his shoulder revealed lots of people gathered at the barrier to watch. No one, however, offered to help.

"Hurry, Phillip!" Steven yelled. "My legs are already in the water."

Phillip was afraid. What could he do? He had to help Steven somehow. He reached out his hand in desperation. He was still two yards away. "Here, grab this ladder," he heard a voice behind him say. He turned around in amazement to see Tai-Kin inching toward him across the ice. Tai-Kin held a long wooden ladder, which he slid toward Phillip. Phillip understood immediately. He grabbed hold of a rung and edged the ladder toward Steven. His heart swelled with relief as Steven grabbed the top rung.

Tension reigned on the ice. Breathlessly, the onlookers watched as Phillip and Tai-Kin gently and slowly pulled the ladder back. Then, the ice beneath Steven broke. The people cried out in shock. Steven held on to the ladder with all his might. And finally, several adults came to help Phillip and Tai-Kin. Together, they pulled Steven back to safety just as two medics came running from the shore.

Only then did Phillip realize that Tai-Kin was wearing neither a coat nor skates. "How did you get here?" he asked, amazed.

Tai-Kin pointed to a house on the shore. "My house," he explained in broken English. "I saw accident from my window, grabbed the ladder, and came to help."

"That was very brave of you." Phillip smiled self-consciously. "Because of you, we saved him."

Phillip pointed to the many people who were watching with great interest as the medics cared for Steven. "None of them helped me." He suddenly had the feeling that words were not adequate for expressing his gratitude to Tai-Kin. "Why don't you come have dinner with us? My mother is making her delicious baked apples for dessert. I'll tell you all about Christmas, and you can tell me about China," he said.

Tai-Kin hesitated at first, and then nodded. "Okay," he said. "Let me get my jacket."

Phillip nodded. "Wait—how do you say 'friend' in Chinese?" he asked.

Tai-Kin paused for a moment. Then he said, "Peng-Yo. Why do you ask?"

Phillip reached out his hand and said, "Peng-Yo?"

Tai-Kin looked at him, a little surprised. Then, he grinned. "Peng-Yo!" he answered, shaking hands.

Pete Smith
THE GIFT

One can never have too many Grandmas—especially around Christmastime. Dominic had five Grandmas: two regular ones, two great-grandmothers, and Grandma Magda, his step-grandmother.

"I get gifts from all of them," Dominic boasted to his friend Gabriel at recess while they watched the girls. "It sure adds up."

"Lucky you," said Gabriel. Gabriel only had one Grandma.

"That's not all, though," Dominic continued. "Do you want to know why?"

Actually, Gabriel could care less. But it didn't look like he had a choice. "Why?"

"Grandpas."

"Don't tell me—you have five, right?"

Just then, Lisa walked by, almost brushing Dominic's arm. "Did you see that?"

"What?"

"I think she likes me."

Gabriel grinned. "You wish!"

That annoyed Dominic a little. Without a word, they walked across the schoolyard, away from the girls. Dominic forgot about the Grandpas again until the bell rang for the next period.

"Yep, Grandpas. I only have two Grandpas, but five Grandmas and two Grandpas makes seven. Plus, one mother and two fathers makes ten . . ."

"Ten gifts," said Gabriel.

"At least," Dominic smiled. "And don't forget aunts and uncles!"

"Cool," said Gabriel, feeling a little better. He had aunts and uncles, too.

After school, Mom peeked in on Dominic as he worked on his homework.

"So, Doc, what do you want for Christmas?"

"From whom?"

"Well, from Stefan and me, of course."

"A computer?" said Dominic.

"Ahhhh, a computer," said his mother before disappearing again.

Did that mean yes or no?

Dominic brought it up again at dinner. "About that computer," he said.

"What computer?" asked Stefan.

"Mom asked me what I wanted for Christmas."

"Oh, I see," said Stefan.

Dominic waited until Stefan had swallowed his

last bite. Then he probed further, "So what do think, Dad?"

Stefan almost choked. That was the first time Dominic had called him Dad.

"We'll think about it," he answered, and Mom nodded.

The next morning at breakfast, Dominic brought it up again. "About that computer . . ."

Before he could finish, his mother held up her hand to stop him. "A computer is an expensive gift, Doc. You realize that, don't you?"

"Maybe all the grandparents could chip in . . . and my other dad, too," he suggested. He'd been awake all night thinking about it.

"We'll think about it. I just don't want you to get your hopes up."

On the way to school, Dominic and Gabriel were squeezed between the older students at the back of the bus.

"I think I'm getting a computer for Christmas!" Dominic shouted.

"Me, too!" Gabriel shouted back.

Dominic grinned at him, "Yeah, right!"

"No, really, it's true," protested Gabriel. "My father's company is buying new ones, and I'm getting my dad's old one."

"Oh, an old one," answered Dominic.

"But to make up for that, they're getting me a printer and a modem to go with it. Will your computer have Internet access?"

"Quit shouting, would you?" Dominic was getting irritated.

Gabriel didn't hear him and went on, "And since almost everything is free, I'm also getting some new software. Isn't that great?"

"Oh yeah, fabulous," said Dominic. Too bad Stefan didn't work for a company like Gabriel's dad.

That afternoon when he got home, his mother asked him to sit down.

"You know, Dominic, Christmas isn't just about getting presents. You're old enough now to be giving gifts of your own to your grandparents this year. I know you don't have a lot of money, but you could make the gifts yourself. I'm sure it would make them happy."

Dominic didn't say anything.

"Oh—and your father would be pleased to receive a little something, too. You know how he is."

That made eight he thought, adding them up. With Mom and Stefan, it was ten. Suddenly he had a lot to do.

Dominic was very busy during the following weeks. He did his homework each day at recess, so he could work on the gifts at home each night. His friend Gabriel was fed up. It wasn't much fun for him to watch girls all by himself.

"I've had it," Gabriel said on the last Monday before Christmas. Dominic sat down after fourth period and opened his math book. "Between your schoolwork and gift-making, you have no time for me anymore. I guess our friendship isn't important?" snapped Gabriel.

"Look," said Dominic, annoyed, "you only have one Grandma you have to give a gift to."

"So? Remember all the gifts you rake in with all your grandparents."

"Whatever," grumbled Dominic. He didn't want to talk about it anymore.

At last, two days before Christmas, all the gifts were finished. Dominic had made calendars for his grandmas and wooden sailboats for his grandpas. Papa Klaus and Stefan were each getting a package of fancy chocolate. He'd bought his mother a sheepskin steering wheel cover. He hoped that everyone would like their gifts.

Finally, Dominic had time for Gabriel again. But when the recess bell rang, his friend was nowhere to be seen. He finally spotted him in the schoolyard. He was standing at the gate with Lisa, chatting up a storm. Dominic was all by himself. I guess Gabe's found a new friend, he thought sadly.

Christmas arrived. "The festival of peace," said Mom, smiling. Of all the Grandmas and the Grandpas, four were spending Christmas with Dominic. Mom and Dominic would visit the others in the days after Christmas.

Dominic was excited. He couldn't wait to give everyone their gifts.

After the huge roast goose dinner, everyone went to stretch out on the couches in the living room. Christmas music was playing softly in the background.

Mom took her time passing out gifts. Each person had to open his or her gift before she moved on to the next person. Dominic's gifts were a huge hit. He was so happy, he almost forgot to open the big box Mom handed him.

"Th-thanks everyone." Dominic was pleased to get the computer he wanted, but he was more pleased that everyone liked the presents he had given them.

"Oh, look—there's one more for you, Doc," said Mom, handing him a second, much smaller gift. He looked questioningly at his grandmas, his grandpas, his mom, and finally at Stefan.

"It's not from any of us," he said. "Someone dropped it off for you."

Dominic grabbed the little package and gave it a squeeze. It felt hard.

There was no gift label on it—only his name written on the wrapping paper.

He ripped it open and pulled out a cell phone.

"Dad," he said out loud. However the card, still in its envelope, was not from his father, but from Lisa.

"Dear Dominic," it read, "Gabriel was nice enough to give me your address. If you like, you can call me during vacation. My number is saved on the phone. Don't wait too long though, because I need it back—I borrowed it. Besides, the battery won't stay charged for long. Merry Christmas, Lisa."

Dominic grinned. And his two grandmas, two grandpas, his mom, and his new father grinned right along with him.

Jonas Torsten Krüger

THE SPIRIT OF CHRISTMAS

Henry and Mike trudged home through the park in the slushy snow. Already dark at four o'clock, the street lamps cast their light onto the grayish path. Henry was the older brother, and Mike believed that Henry knew everything.

"What do you want for Christmas, Henry?" asked Mike when the evening stillness became too much for him.

Henry happily began reciting his list, "First, that new robot wars video game."

"Awesome! That's a really awesome game, isn't it?" Awesome was Mike's favorite word.

"Mmmm-hmmm. And then I'd like a cell phone, an MP3 player, and, of course, the new Turbo Max Sled."

"Awesome," repeated Mike and pointed straight ahead. "Hey, look at that old guy! What's wrong with him?"

An old man stood in the circle of light cast by a lamp. He had only a white band of hair around his ears, and a dirty brown gown covering his thin body.

"Don't know," said Henry, but as they continued walking, it seemed to get a little darker.

As they got closer, they noticed that the man held his hand outstretched, palm up. A tiny bird with its feathers all puffed up was perched there.

"I guess he's just feeding the birds," said Henry, relieved.

When they tried to walk past the old man, he looked at them. "Good evening, Mike, Henry," he said nodding at them.

Shocked, the brothers stopped. How did he know their names?

"Might you two have a few crumbs for my friend here?"

Peep, confirmed the small bird.

"Sorry, no. Only chewing gum." Mike popped his.

The man shrugged his shoulders sadly and took a step toward them. "Did you know that this is a chickadee?" he asked. "There are black-capped, mountain, boreal, and chestnut-backed chickadees."

The brothers leaned forward hesitantly to look at the bird. Mike whispered quietly to his brother, "He's a real bird freak, isn't he?"

Henry paid no attention. Instead, he glanced back and forth between the bird and the man's face. He had so many wrinkles! He had furrows on his forehead, deep creases on his neck, and big wrinkles on his cheeks.

Slowly, he asked, "Who are you? And how old are you?"

The man interrupted him with a chuckle. "My name is Francis and I guess you would agree I'm old—very old."

Francis gently stroked the chickadee, which sat patiently in his palm.

Strange, thought Henry—what made the bird perch there so quietly? Just then, a second bird fluttered over, circled once, and also settled on his hand. It was a little bigger than the first chickadee, dirty yellow, with a black-and-white head.

Snap, pop, went Mike's chewing gum. "Birds are boring," said Mike.

The old man looked at the brothers for a long time. Though his lips no longer laughed, his eyes twinkled all the more. "Boring? But it's so easy to enjoy them."

"Nah," Henry shook his head.

"It's true," insisted Francis. "They are such beautiful animals. Their feathery coats are beautiful, and so is their silvery song."

He blew gently upon the bird's tiny feathers.

"Boring," Mike maintained. "It's not like you can talk to them or anything."

Henry couldn't figure this guy out.

Francis observed the boys, his smile now entirely gone from his lips. Instead, a bright light shone from his eyes, burning like a New Year's Eve sparkler. "You think they're boring, that they can't talk?" he said, his voice hoarse. "Then listen closely."

Francis carefully cupped his hands around both birds, swung them up into the air, and let them fly. He stood with his thin fingers outstretched and the boys began to hear a vibrating and rattling sound. Henry shook his head. The birds above them twittered excitedly. And suddenly, Henry and Mike began—yes, they began to hear.

Suddenly they understood the blackbird's wistful warbling, calling for spring. They heard the magpie's chatter, telling the tale of the silver spoon it had pilfered. They heard the woodpecker drilling its hunger into a tree trunk, the sparrows telling each other jokes, and the robin singing of love. They also heard the little chickadee chirping to itself. It was worried about whether it would find a good nesting place in the spring.

Mike forgot to chew his gum.

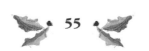

Chickadee   Robin   Magpie

Henry tugged his ear in disbelief. And Francis, the old man in the brown robes, smiled, folding his fingers back together and letting his arms return to his sides.

As quickly as it had started, it stopped, and the birds' conversation turned back to their normal birdsong.

"Awesome," whispered Mike. Henry pulled him back—he was a little scared by the whistling and trilling and twittering all around him.

"You have to go home now," said Francis.

"Yes, right! Come on, Mike. Hurry up!"

"What's the rush, Henry?"

"I . . . I have to change my wish list! Goodbye!"

And the two boys ran off, passing under the light of the street lamps before being completely swallowed by the night's darkness.

Francis of Assisi watched them go as he smoothed his monk's habit. For what new things would the boy wish? Francis smiled— that had been fun! He was already looking forward to the next December 12—his Name

Day—when he was allowed to walk among people once again.

Smiling, he waved farewell to his fluttering friends—and disappeared into the air.

At home, Henry took out his wish list, crossed out the robot wars video game, and replaced it with birdhouse.

Gerda Anger-Schmidt
MOM GOES ON STRIKE

No one could have predicted that Mom would go on strike at Christmastime.

It all started innocently enough the first Sunday in Advent. Mom had made a list of all the people she had to send Christmas cards to this year. Dad was in the kitchen cooking. MiniMo, my little brother, was writing a letter—a top secret letter, he said. But it wasn't too secret—I could hear him reading the words aloud as he wrote "Dear Santa . . ." I was practicing some Christmas songs on the piano. Grandma was due to arrive any minute, and then we were going to have our little Advent celebration.

"Hey, where is Ben?" asked MiniMo abruptly.

"That lazy lump is still asleep," said Mom. She didn't sound pleased at all. Ben is our big brother and is almost seventeen. He's constantly fighting with our parents. Most of their arguments have to do with his weird hairstyles. He had a Mohawk last summer, dreadlocks in the fall, and, at the moment, he is completely bald.

There he was at the door, pale and thin as a rail. He complained about a headache and asked Mom for an aspirin.

"Poor Ben!" said MiniMo sympathetically. He climbed down from his chair to help Ben to the sofa as if he were seriously ill. "There. Make yourself comfortable!" MiniMo adored Ben, and would do anything to help him feel better. Ben had given MiniMo his nickname, which was short for Mini-Monster, but even that didn't get MiniMo upset. In fact, if you called him by his real name, Manuel, he'd ignore you.

Mom got a glass of water and an aspirin. "Let me tell you, Ben, if you get me out of bed after midnight one more time because you've forgotten your keys, then . . ."

"I'll let you in," MiniMo whispered to him.

"I was trying to call Dad so I wouldn't wake you," Ben defended himself.

"Oh, please," said Mom. "You know perfectly well that bulldozers couldn't wake him once he's in bed asleep!"

As if on cue, Dad poked his head through the doorway. "Umm, I still need a few gifts for our employees," he said to Mom. "Do you think you could pick them up, honey? The Christmas party is at the end of the week."

He spotted Ben. "Ahhh, His Highness is up!" Dad's voice got serious. "Better put on a hat before Grandma arrives. I'd rather not have to discuss your baldness with her."

Ben glanced at Dad with a pained expression. He pulled an old Santa hat from his pocket and pulled it over his head.

"Happy?" he asked.

Dad mumbled something and retreated back into the kitchen.

In his high voice, MiniMo sang, "Santa Claus Is Coming to Town." I accompanied him on the piano. Ben chimed in with made-up lyrics: "We're getting a pet / With lots of black spots / He's worth ten thousand dollars / and we'll go where he trots / Santa Claus is bringing a horse!"

The doorbell rang, and Ben shot up off the couch. "That would be Grandma! Come on, MiniMo!" The two raced to the door. I followed on their heels.

"Hi, Grandma!" We took her coat and hat while she held tightly to the Advent wreath, which she brings with her each year. She wanted to carry it into the living room herself, as if she were afraid we would break it.

Dinner went smoothly without any major incidents. I told her about being the angel in our nativity play. "And I'm going to be a sheep," said MiniMo. His whole face glowed.

"And I will be dear little Jesus," said Ben sarcastically.

"Ben!" Dad glared at him.

"Just joking!" mumbled Ben.

"You can be the ox *and* the donkey," I sneered. I didn't like it when he made fun of our nativity play.

"Children, children, enough fighting!" Grandma tried to calm us down.

After dinner, Dad lit the first candle on the Advent wreath. I played a few Christmas songs.

The others sang along—Mom with her hoarse soprano, MiniMo high pitched and off-key, Ben mute, with his mouth opening and closing like a fish, and Dad with his booming bass. Grandma was so touched she couldn't get a note out.

Grandma complained about her arthritis and all the things she still had to do before Christmas. She asked Mom if she could run a few errands for her. She needed some gifts, some baked goods, and some new Christmas tree decorations. Oh, and it would be wonderful if Mom would buy a few cards for her sisters, write the cards, and then bring them by so Grandma could sign them herself.

Mom gasped for air. "William could take care of the cards for you!" she said, glaring at Dad.

"But, dear, William already has his hands full with work!" Grandma came to her son's defense. "Besides, you have nicer handwriting. You also have more time."

"Your mother seems to think that I have nothing better to do then run errands and write out cards," snapped Mom after Grandma left. Mom was pretty upset.

"But, darling, she didn't mean any harm. Sometimes, it is simply too much for her, especially right before Christmas."

"Okay, time to make myself scarce," said Ben, taking off his hat. "All this fuss about Christmas is lame."

"Lame?" repeated Mom slowly.

Ben was already out the door. He swung back around, "Yup, lame. By the way, is it okay if I go to a party the day after Christmas?"

"Ben, you know that's the day we go to your uncle Fred's," Dad chimed in. "It's a tradition."

"Who needs tradition?" Ben shot back. "It's always the same boring people having the same boring conversations. It's totally lame."

He started to leave the room, but Mom stood in his way.

"Just a moment, Ben!" she said. "Maybe you're right. Maybe there really is no meaning left in those things we call tradition which seem so lame to you. Maybe we should just forget about Christmas this year."

Ben's jaw dropped in amazement. "No Christmas tree? No visits to relatives?"

"Exactly."

"Hey, cool!" Ben was impressed. "Really cool! Wait until my friends hear about this!"

"No Christmas carp?" asked MiniMo hopefully, since he hated fish.

"No Christmas carp," confirmed Mom.

"Cool!" said MiniMo, impressed. "Really cool!

I have to tell my kindergarten class."

"No tree, no carp?" asked Dad, dismayed. "No traditions at all? We can't do that to Grandma!"

"Especially since it also seems to be tradition that I have to juggle everything by *my*self," said Mom, "and every year there's more and more added to *my* to-do-list, and no one ever offers to help. Christmas should be about much more than that!"

Embarrassed, Dad, Ben, and I were quiet— at least until MiniMo suddenly sat up, breaking the silence with the words of the angel, "Behold! I bring you tidings of great joy."

The third week of Advent had already begun, and Mom was still serious about her Christmas boycott. She didn't lift a finger with respect to Christmas preparations. "No stress, no hustle and bustle," she said over and over. "I am enjoying this!"

That's because the rest of us were busy getting stressed—well at least Dad, Ben, and I.

Dad had to buy his employees' gifts himself.

He wrote out all of our Christmas cards and Grandma's, too. He also promised to take care of the tree. It wouldn't do to be completely without a tree.

It also wouldn't do to completely forget about the Christmas baking. Even Ben agreed on that point. Skipping too many traditions is lame, he said.

Since Dad once told me that a good manager must delegate, I gave Ben the assignment of 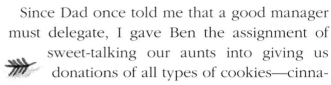 sweet-talking our aunts into giving us donations of all types of cookies—cinnamon stars, rum balls, and vanilla crescents. As long as he poured on the charm, I figured we would get a decent amount of goodies.

And because I knew all about how forgetful Dad can be, I called my godfather to ask him for a Christmas tree, just in case. If he couldn't get us one, I'd ask our school janitor for the tree from the auditorium.

And as for that MiniMo—he learned the entire nativity play by heart! Perhaps I could even delegate my part to him. After all, who would care if one of the angels was on the short side?

And so it was, the Christmas when Mom went on strike.

MEMORY PAGES

Here is space for more of your holiday memories!

MEMORY PAGES

MEMORY PAGES

MEMORY PAGES

Andreas Schlüter

YOU DO BELIEVE IN GUINEA PIGS, DON'T YOU?

Sasha was desperate. There were only eleven days until Christmas Eve and she still didn't have any presents for her parents. It was their fault though—they could buy themselves anything they wanted, and they did! There wasn't a thing that they did not already own. Sasha had no idea at all about what she could get them.

There was, of course, one obvious solution—the homemade gift. Sasha knew all about those. She had already given them something homemade for the past five Christmases and for their birthdays, too. Her parents now owned carved letter openers, paperweights made from chiselled stone, clay coffee mugs, crocheted potholders, a photo calendar, painted signs for the kitchen, shower, bathroom, and front door, printed T-shirts, painted silk scarves, folded paper lampshades, and embroidered handkerchiefs. All handmade by her. At this point, Sasha could practically host her own television craft series. But now she had run out of ideas.

"Ha," she heard from somewhere.

Sasha had heard it very clearly. It sounded like a short, dry, mocking laugh. Even though she was alone, she looked all around. But she didn't see anyone.

She sat at her desk, her chin propped on her hands.

"Out of ideas. Unbelievable," announced the voice.

Sasha was positive she heard it. Someone had spoken to her. The voice sounded high, shrill, and squeaky. If guinea pigs could talk, that's what they would sound like, she thought.

The voice seemed to come from under her desk. She bent down, and sure enough—a small guinea pig with brown and white spots was huddled right there! Sasha had always wished for one just like this. But her parents didn't allow pets. First of all, because pets were dirty, and second, well, "because I say so," said her father.

"Are you talking to me?" she asked.

"Of course!" answered the guinea pig.

"Who are you?" asked Sasha.

"Can't you see? I'm a guinea pig?" came the defiant answer.

"What's your name? How did you get here?" she asked.

"How am *I* supposed to know?" the guinea pig exclaimed.

The guinea pig must have come from somewhere. She was quite sure it hadn't been born under her desk. And who, besides the guinea pig, would know how it had gotten there.

"Obviously you have no imagination," grum-

bled the guinea pig. "None at all!"

Enough! She had wanted a guinea pig, but not one like this. She had wanted a guinea pig that was cuddly and cute and lovable, not a back-talking one with a bad attitude.

"What are you so mad about?" she asked. "I have enough to worry about. Perhaps you should just go away!"

"Ha!" laughed the guinea pig. "You must be kidding me. Do you think I have nothing better to do? You're the one who forced me to come here!"

Astounded, Sasha gaped at the guinea pig. What was that supposed to mean?

"Look around your room," said the guinea pig.

Sasha looked around, but didn't see anything special. Her room was the same as it always was. Nothing seemed out of the ordinary.

"Look at the pictures!" said the guinea pig, sighing heavily, as though it were a great burden for him to have to explain everything to her.

Sasha looked carefully at the pictures she had drawn and tacked up on her walls. As she examined them, she stuck her head under the desk to get a good look at the guinea pig.

How odd! It looked exactly like the one in her drawings.

She leafed through her pictures. Some of them had word balloons coming from the guinea pig's mouth. The guinea pig was saying rude things to her father, who had rejected the purchase of a guinea pig *because I say so.*

"You see!" stated the guinea pig. "That is how you wished me to be, and that is how I turned out."

Sasha was so surprised her mouth fell wide open. "Do you mean that . . ."

"Sure!" confirmed the guinea pig. "What did you think? *I* am the product of *your* imagination!"

Now it was Sasha who had to laugh. The lively, talking guinea pig sitting right in front of her nose was the product of her imagination? How ridiculous!

"Okay, let's say you're right," Sasha admitted. "What does this have to do with gifts for my parents?"

The guinea pig came out from under the desk. He walked over to an empty cardboard box, which lay on the floor. Sasha had intended to use it to store her colored pencils.

"Just use your imagination," suggested the guinea pig.

This was about the stupidest thing she'd ever heard. She couldn't give her parents an empty cardboard box for Christmas!

The guinea pig looked at her, and, suddenly, Sasha understood. She watched in amazement as the guinea pig paled and then disappeared completely.

Eleven days later, it was time. Sasha was excited as all children are just before the gifts are distributed. But this year, it was not because of the anticipation about what she would receive, but because she could hardly wait to see her parents' reaction to the gift she was giving them.

Same as every year, Mother rang a little bell when Sasha was allowed to enter the festive, candle-lit living room. Father focused his digital video camera on the gifts under the magnificently decorated Christmas tree. He expected Sasha to dive right into the pile of beautiful, glittering packages. Instead, she remained standing in the middle of the room, her hands hidden behind her back.

Mother turned to Sasha, concerned, "What's the matter darling? Don't you want to open your gifts?"

Sasha pulled a package out from behind her back, shyly handing it to her mother. "This is for both of you," she said.

Confused, Mother accepted the package—they had a family tradition that adults waited to open their presents until after the children had received theirs. She gave her husband a puzzled glance as he continued filming everything. "Why, thank you, Sasha!" she managed to say at last.

"Come on, open it!" urged Sasha, who couldn't stand the suspense a minute longer.

Mother opened the package and peered into the empty cardboard box. Father put down the camera, came closer, and stared inside. "What is it?" they asked.

"A trip to a tropical island!" declared Sasha. Her parents still looked confused They looked at their daughter with concern and surprise. She dashed to the stereo, turned off the Christmas CD that was playing, and replaced it with some calypso music. Before either had a chance to say a word, they had colored paper leis around their necks. Sasha blew out the Christmas candles and flipped two switches, bathing the room in the bright yellow of two sunlamps.

"Haven't you always wanted to go to the tropics?" asked Sasha as she breezed past her completely dumbfounded parents.

"Uh, sure . . ." her father managed to say. "But you know that I don't have any vacation time right now because . . ."

"Wrong!" said Sasha. "You are already on vacation!"

She had a big plastic basket in her hand, that she emptied out at her parents' feet. All sorts of stuffed exotic animals landed on the carpet: crocodiles, parrots, a hippopotamus, several snakes, a zebra, and even a tarantula.

Mother looked around the living room, which no longer looked the slightest bit Christmasy. Instead of Christmas tunes, calypso music blared through the living room. The Christmas candles were out, and the palms glowed. Everyone wore colorful paper flower leis, and a pile of exotic stuffed animals lay at their feet. Sasha handed her parents water wings, flippers, and swim goggles. After that, she spread two bath towels on the floor and dragged in an inflatable plastic island with a palm tree.

"What is this for?" her father managed to ask just as Sasha asked them to shut their eyes and sit on the towels.

It took a little convincing on Sasha's part before her parents gave in. With closed eyes, goggles on their faces, and flippers on their feet, they sat down on the bath towels in the living room.

Sasha stood there for a moment. Her parents still didn't quite seem to understand. That was obvious to her. She wondered whether she should dare to continue to the highlight of the evening. But, she had nothing to lose. It would either work, or it wouldn't.

Sasha reminded them to keep their eyes shut. When she finally allowed her parents to reopen their eyes, Mother shrieked in horror and Father rubbed his eyes, as if he were dreaming.

Sasha had poured several buckets of sand around the plastic island, right in the middle of the living room carpet.

"Sasha, what on earth are you doing!" Mother cried out, jumping up from the towel. Her husband held her back. He dug his hand into the sand and said in surprise, "This is fine sand, just like at the beach!"

Sasha beamed. Her father understood. Mother's face glowed dark red. She was thinking about how many hours it would take to clean up the sand. "Are you nuts?" she asked. Sasha didn't know if Mother was referring to her or to her father.

Father made a calming hand motion, picked up his video camera, turned on the zoom, and showed his wife the scene on the fold-out screen.

"What?" asked Mother, irritated.

Only the sand, the island, a few stuffed animals, and a sand pail, which Sasha had stuck into the sand, were visible on the screen.

"Look, it really is a tropical island!" said Father.

Sasha's mother looked at her husband with a combination of pity and anger. "Really!" she repeated, scathingly.

Father nodded, grinning.

"Since we can't go on a vacation to a tropical island, Sasha brought the island to us. Look." Again, he showed her the screen.

"A tropical island?" asked Mother once more. Sasha noticed clearly that her voice sounded much gentler.

"Exactly!" cried Sasha joyfully. She went into the kitchen to get the juice she had pre-pared for them. "It's pineapple, orange, and banana, with coconut flakes on top. Very tropical!"

Smiling, her parents let their daughter serve them. "Cheers!" they said, raising their glasses to her.

"What are we going to do on this island?" asked Mother.

Father laughed and sprang up. He returned to the room a minute later. "Why, we'll put on some of this, of course," he called, holding a bottle of sunblock. "We'd better, in this heat!"

Mother still couldn't believe it. She hesitated, threw a quick, longing glance at the dark Christmas tree, thought better of it, stood up, too, and left the room. For a moment, Sasha feared she wasn't going to return.

Then her mother came back—in her swimsuit! She grabbed the lotion from her husband's hand and began to apply it. To her husband and Sasha, she said, "You guys are crazy, sitting there fully dressed at the beach!"

Sasha and Father laughed, before going off to change into swimsuits, too. When they came back, they all danced in the sand to the calypso music.

"This is just marvelous!" said Mother, relaxing on her back. "Just think. Here we are on Christmas, basking in the warm tropical sun, while everyone else is freezing at home!"

"Exactly!" Father agreed. He put on his sunglasses, ended the dance with his daughter, and lay down on the towel next to Mother. He gave her a kiss and whispered, "We have our daughter to thank for this wonderful tropical vacation!"

Sasha beamed, drizzled a little bit of the fine sand over her mother's leg, and announced, "I forgot the best part of all—I've booked the entire week!"

Mother and Father grinned at each other. They wondered how the grandparents would react to their surprise trip to the tropics tomorrow.

Sasha reassured her parents, "Don't worry, I booked beach chairs for them, too!"

Sabine Dillner
CHRISTMAS MAGIC

Laurence lived with his mother in an apartment in the city. It was a morning before Christmas break, and, as usual, Laurence was late for school.

"Bye, Mom!" he said. He had to get to school. "Have a good day!"

"You too, sweetheart!" his mother said.

Just as he started out the door, she put her finger on her lips and pulled him back. A door closed downstairs. Quiet as mice, Laurence and his mother waited until Mr. Schulz had left the building. Mr. Schulz lived directly below them and always complained about the noise from upstairs.

"Mr. Schulz is such a sad person," his mother had told him. "He lives all by himself. No one ever visits him . . ."

Laurence wasn't surprised. After all, only a crazy person would willingly go visit that nasty man.

When Laurence came home from school, he found a girl sitting in front of their door. She looked like she was eight or nine years old.

"Hey!" said Laurence, puzzled. "What are you doing here?"

The girl stood up. "I've come to see you," she announced cheerfully. "My grandma told me to look for someone who could explain Christmas to me. I bet you know all about Christmas."

Embarrassed, Laurence shrugged his shoulders. He took a closer look at her. She had a round face, light, yellow-green eyes, and red braids that hung over her shoulders. Her dress looked like it had been sewn together from scraps. He hoped she wasn't a runaway or an escapee from a mental institution.

"What's your name?" asked the girl. "I'm Charlotte. Do you like that name?"

"Of course, yes, that's a very nice name." Laurence thought for a moment. "Where do you live? Are you lost?"

"I'm supposed to go to your apartment," insisted Charlotte, "and wait there until Grandma picks me up."

"But how will your grandma know where you are?"

"Oh, she can find me anywhere," she said.

Now he was certain that she was crazy. He should call the police right away, so that someone could come and take care of her.

It probably wasn't a good idea to let a strange girl into the apartment, but he couldn't leave her out here in the stairwell, where she might wander off and get hurt.

Laurence unlocked the door. "Come on in!" he said.

Charlotte walked past him. "Where are all your evergreen branches and red candles?" she asked disappointedly.

"Grandma says that every home is decorated for Christmas now, and that I should look at all the decorations. Maybe you could sing me a Christmas carol? And what about that roast goose? Grandma says . . ." She interrupted her chatter and peered under the bed. "Where is your cat?"

"We don't have a cat. If we had a pet, old Mr. Schulz would probably get us evicted."

"Who is old Mr. Schulz?" asked Charlotte curiously. "Is he a troll or something? They can be pretty disgusting. Perhaps he ate your cat. Hmmmm," she said thoughtfully, "don't worry, I'm here now, and I'm good at dealing with trolls." She sprang up and danced around the room with her arms stretched out. "Yoo-hoo, Mr. Tro-ollll—come out, come out, wherever you are!" she sang, stamping her feet.

"Shhh! Be quiet—please! Do you hear that?" Laurence held her by the arm and pointed to the floor.

Just as Laurence had feared, Mr. Schulz was already knocking from below with the end of his broom. "Great! Now I'm really in trouble!"

"Oh, okay, I'll be quiet. Really, I will. I promise on my grandma's horns!" Charlotte laughed mischievously. "Just kidding! Of course, my grandma doesn't have horns."

This Charlotte was really a piece of work. Laurence hoped she would be quiet now. Where was she? Good grief! What was she doing in the bathroom? Laurence hesitated and then put his ear to the door. He heard water splashing—and it was splashing on the floor.

Laurence ripped the door open. "What are you doing?" he yelled.

"Making rain," Charlotte explained proudly. The showerhead sprayed water all over the bathroom. Laurence dove to the faucet and turned it off. He tore towels from their hooks and threw them onto the floor. "Quick! Help me! We have to mop this up right away!" he yelled as he wrung the sopping wet towels out over the sink.

Someone was ringing the doorbell. And then a fist hammered on the door.

"Open up immediately or I'll call the police!" Laurence's whole body trembled. "Th . . . th . . . that's Mr. . . . . Mr . . ."

Charlotte puffed disdainfully. "Oh brother!" she said, snapping her fingers. The bathroom was dry in a second, with the towels neatly hung on their hooks. "Fine, if he really wants to come in so badly, we'll let him in," she finally said, hopping to the door and opening it.

Mr. Schulz barreled past her, his face beet red. "The ceiling is dripping in my bathroom. Just wait till I get my hands on you!" he yelled.

Laurence stared at Mr. Schulz in disbelief. Mr. Schulz had been transformed into Santa Claus, complete with a white beard and red coat. Santa looked just as shocked as Laurence. He held his hand to his throat and croaked, as though he were choking. Then he opened his mouth and said, "I've brought you a little Christmas cheer. You spend too much time alone. I bet you could use a little company . . ." He held out a tiny, white kitten.

"I—uh—thank you!" stammered Laurence.

Santa Schulz walked out the door without a word. When he reached the stairs, he turned around, but he'd already turned back into Mr. Schulz, only his face was no longer red. Now it was chalky white. "Got to move someplace else . . ." Laurence heard him mutter to himself as he stumbled down the stairs.

Laurence glanced from the kitten in his arms to Charlotte. "How did you do that?"

"Wasn't it great?" asked Charlotte innocently. She went to the window and looked up at the sky. "My grandma will be here any minute."

Laurence stood next to her and looked up at the sky as well. It had begun to snow. "It's going to be pretty cold on that broom," he said.

"Broom?" said Charlotte scornfully. "What *are* you talking about? Well, I have to go now. It was nice meeting you, Laurence. Merry Christmas! I'm sure we'll see each other again sometime."

Before Laurence could say a word, she had disappeared out the door.

"Thank goodness!" said Laurence's mother when Mr. Schulz moved out the very next day. "I hope someone nice moves into that apartment now."

On the day before Christmas, Laurence saw an old woman in the stairwell. She wore a long dress, which looked as though it were made from scraps that had been pieced together. Friendly, yellow-green eyes peered out from her wrinkly, round face.

"You must be Laurence," she said. "Would you help us carry our things up?"

"Carry?" asked Laurence. "Why don't you just use magic to get them upstairs?"

The old woman laughed. "Where did you get *that* crazy idea from?" she asked, winking at him.

Laurence's mother leaned over the railing. "A girl named Charlotte is waiting for you up here. She and her grandma are moving in downstairs. Perhaps our new neighbors would like to spend Christmas with us tomorrow."

"What a great idea, Mom!" Laurence was thrilled.

It looked like Christmas might be pretty good after all!

Sabine Streufert
CAROLINE'S GUARDIAN ANGEL

"Caroline, are you ready? We have to go!" Caroline's parents were putting on their coats in the hallway.

"I don't want to go," she said quietly, looking out the window. It was drizzling outside. Despite the festive holiday lights, the streets looked dull and dismal.

"Caroline!" called her father, a little louder this time.

Caroline sighed. She had always enjoyed the time before Christmas. But, everything was different this year. It would be her first Christmas without Grandpa. She felt the tears welling up in her eyes.

"Caroline, where are you?" Her parents were getting impatient.

"I'm coming!" She wiped her eyes with the back of her hand.

Grandpa had been her best friend. He had always been there when she needed him. Caroline felt a telltale tear slip down her cheek.

"Caroline, we have to go *now*!" Her mother was standing directly behind her. Caroline hadn't heard her coming. "Oh, honey, you're crying." She gently held Caroline in her arms. "You miss him, don't you?"

"It's okay. I'm on my way down." Caroline slipped out of her mother's arms and hurried down the stairs.

"Let's go, we don't want to miss the concert," Caroline's mother said enthusiastically. A concert! Caroline rolled her eyes.

The shopping district was already packed with people. Caroline and her parents were swept along by the crowds. Lots of people were already waiting for the concert to begin. "I'd like to look around a little bit," she said hoping that the market would be less busy during the concert.

"All right, but be back in one hour and stay inside the market."

Typical Mom, she always worried too much. "I'm eleven—not a baby anymore." Caroline sighed and stormed off. Sure enough, the market was a bit emptier. Booths sold hot chocolate, Christmas cookies, candles, and jewelry. There was even an old-fashioned carousel, a Christmas tree lot, and, of course, a Santa Claus.

Those men in Santa suits are for kids, thought Caroline wearily and trudged on. Suddenly, something familiar surfaced between the heads of the shoppers in front of her. That hat! Wasn't that? Caroline's heart leaped to her throat. There! There it was again! It was a dark blue cap. Grandpa! Even though she knew it couldn't really be true, she found herself speeding up, but suddenly it disappeared.

Not knowing what to do, Caroline stopped.

"Who were you chasing, little girl?"

The two boys, who looked about fifteen years old, were speaking to her. "Hey, are you deaf or something?" They came closer. Caroline felt uncomfortable and took a few steps back. "Nice purse you have there. Let's see how much money your mommy sent us." The bigger of the two boys reached for her purse.

"No," screamed Caroline. She turned around and ran, the two boys on her heels. She turned and slipped through a gap between the booths and kept running. Suddenly, the path came to a dead end! Caroline looked around anxiously, but there was no escape. She was trapped. The boys had already caught up to her.

"Bad luck, little girl." The older one grinned. "Time to pay up."

Caroline's heart was racing in fear. Her hand gripped her purse tightly.

"Hand it over." The boys slowly came closer. Caroline wanted to cry for help, but fear closed her throat. "Well, fine. Have it your way . . . Hey! What?"

A man stood behind the boys, gripping them by the hoods of their jackets. Caroline could hardly believe her eyes. The man wore a blue cap. "Leave the girl alone," she heard him say.

"Otherwise, you'll have to deal with me. Don't you have anything better to do than to steal money from an eleven-year-old girl?"

The two boys looked at each other, appalled. They quickly freed themselves from the man's grasp and ran away.

"Are you all right?" the man asked, concerned. The deep voice sounded familiar.

"Yes . . . I'm, uh, fine, thanks," she stammered as she tried to get a look at the man's face. But it was too dark behind the booths to see anything clearly.

"Good, then let's go back." The man accompanied Caroline back through the booths, and then he was gone. Where could he have gone? She turned around and looked in every direction. It was strange how he'd shown up just in the nick of time and even stranger that he knew her age.

She could just hear the brass ensemble playing "Silent Night, Holy Night." That meant the concert was almost over.

"Merry Christmas!" said a voice near Caroline, startling her. The costumed Santa Claus was offering her a candy cane. "Sorry, I didn't mean to make you jump! You look as though you've seen a ghost," he said when he saw the look on her face.

"No, not a ghost," said Caroline. She thought quietly for a moment, and then it came to her. Of course! It had to be. She was sure of it. A little smile danced at the edges of her mouth. "Just my guardian angel!"

Margret Rettich
AN AWFUL STORY

This story isn't awful just because Mom and Aunt Marie couldn't stand each other. It is true that Aunt Marie was sometimes difficult. And, she had made trouble for Mom a while ago, but Mom had long forgotten about it.

This story isn't awful just because Dad had a hard time shopping for presents each year. Many men have that problem, and Mom understood. She would buy gifts for the entire family, including Aunt Marie. Dad was grateful for this.

No, this story is awful because Dad went to visit Aunt Marie shortly before Christmas and because of a trash collection day and because Mom . . . but, first things first.

The thing is, Aunt Marie was crazy about Dad. When he was in college, he lived at her house and she waited on him hand and foot. So when he brought his girlfriend home to meet her, it just wasn't going to go well. Aunt Marie was jealous. She listened at the door, peeped through the keyhole, and forbade visits after ten o'clock at night. And she warned Dad about *that* woman. Thankfully, Dad didn't allow himself to be misled, and he married Mom despite the warnings.

Aunt Marie still loved to spoil Dad when he visited. She'd make his favorite foods and bring out the photo albums and talk about the good old days. Each time he visited, she'd give him a little gift. Usually it was something sweet. Dad loved sweets and Aunt Marie felt sorry for him because Mom always had him on a diet.

Aunt Marie was ill last fall. When he visited, Dad was shocked to see how old she looked and how small she had become. When he left, she gave him a tiny little box. It was wrapped in red paper and tied with a gold bow.

"This time, it's not for you," she said. "It is for your wife."

As he drove home, Dad shook the box and held it to his ear. There was something small and hard inside. It occurred to him that Aunt Marie had not been wearing the brooch she usually wore. Now, he could have given Mom the box right away. But Christmas was only a few weeks off. If he saved the box from Aunt Marie, at least this year, he'd have a present for Mom that she didn't buy for herself.

All Dad needed was a hiding place. Easier said than done. Mom knew every corner of our house. There was only one room in the basement that she rarely went into, it was just too messy for her—Dad's workshop. And that was where the old, rickety bureau stood. Dad used it to store his tools. It even had a secret compartment—well, kind of a secret compartment. Dad had put a second bottom on it after a family of mice gnawed a hole into the bureau and had set up house in a nest of oil rags. Perfect!

So Dad slid the little box between the two bottoms. Mom would definitely not find it there. Then he went upstairs for dinner. "Aunt Marie said to say Merry Christmas," he said as he sat down to eat.

So far, this is a perfectly normal story. But here comes the awful part.

A few weeks passed, and the Christmas spirit was everywhere. Wreaths decorated doors, Christmas lights glowed on houses, and icicle lights framed windows. Mom baked a ridiculous amount of cookies. She sent some along with Dad when he went to visit Aunt Marie. Lukas went along this time. He usually avoided these visits like Mom did, but Aunt Marie had given him some money last year, and it seemed the least he could do to thank her. Besides, she might want to give him something again this year.

They drank tea with Aunt Marie and munched Mom's cookies. When they left, Aunt Marie gave Dad a box of chocolate and Lukas got some money. Then, Aunt Marie kissed them both, and Dad and Lukas drove home.

As they came around the corner, they discovered a heavily laden station wagon blocking their driveway. Dad honked furiously. The station wagon drove off and disappeared. Even though it was dark, Lukas had seen Dad's bureau among the rest of the junk in the back of the station wagon.

When Lukas mentioned this to Dad, he got a panicky look on his face. "You've got to be kidding me," he said.

Unfortunately, as Dad soon learned, Lukas had not been kidding. In front of the house, Mom was busily piling up old garden chairs, trash bags, the broken lawnmower, and the snow shovel that was missing its handle. "Those guys turn everything upside down.

They pick through the junk, take what they like, and leave the rest a mess," she scolded.

"Why did they take Dad's bureau?" asked Lukas.

"That ugly thing had to go. That's why I set it out," said Mom, as she kicked the snow shovel. "I'm giving Dad a new tool chest for Christmas. But don't tell him!" she whispered to Lukas.

Mom went into the house.

"Did she just say my bureau is gone?" he raced to the basement. He was back in no time.

"Come on! Let's go!" he said, sounding agitated. He jumped back into the car. Lukas had barely climbed into the seat next to him before Dad started the engine and threw the car into reverse. They almost ran over Mom, who was adding a suitcase to the trash pile. She called something after them, but they couldn't hear what she said as they sped around the corner. As Dad drove along the street, he peered down the side streets, repeating, "We have to find that station wagon. We must get that bureau back!"

"Forget about that old bureau," said Lukas. "It was falling apart anyway."

Dad did not reply. With great determination, he drove down one street after the next. He finally spotted the jam-packed station wagon, almost at the edge of the city. Dad sped up and almost rammed into it when it stopped suddenly in front of a house. Three men climbed out and began combing through the pile of trash that lay there. They didn't see Dad get out of his car. He was trying to yank the bureau out of their vehicle. With Lukas's help, he had almost succeeded when one of the men discovered them. He yelled at Dad in an unintelligible language. Then, all three men leaped into the station wagon and took off.

Dad shoved Lukas into the car and followed them in wild pursuit out beyond the city limits. It was pure luck that there were no cars coming the other way.

"Dad, why do you want that old bureau back anyway?" asked Lukas, hanging onto the door handle for dear life as the car careened around another corner.

"I don't," said Dad in reply. He didn't say more. Meanwhile, the station wagon had left the road and was driving down a dirt path. Dad followed behind.

This time, the men were waiting for him. With legs planted apart, they stood in the dark shadows of the headlights. Dad got out and walked toward them, his hands raised. Just like in the movies, thought

Lukas. All Dad needed was a white cloth to wave.

"Please, no fighting," said Dad.

It turned out that two of the men spoke English rather well, so Dad dealt with them. He told them that he wanted to buy the bureau back from them. They declined, but offered him the other junk they had picked up. Dad did not want any of that. He gave them first one, then two, and finally three large bills. Finally they had a deal and the bureau was unloaded. The men climbed back into their station wagon and drove away.

"Why did you want that old bureau back?" asked Lukas for the third time, almost revealing that Dad was getting a new tool chest for Christmas.

"I'll tell you later," said Dad. "Help me carry this." They dragged the bureau to the car and lifted it into the trunk. It stuck so far out that Dad had to tie down the tailgate with a rope. They drove back to the road with the bureau swaying and the tailgate bouncing up and down.

"We're going to lose the bureau by the time we get home, Dad" said Lukas.

Dad grunted. He stopped at the side of the road and got out. He heaved the bureau out of the trunk. Then, in the beam of the headlights, he started to smash it using the car jack.

Bewildered, Lukas called out, "Dad, what are you doing?"

Dad didn't answer. That's when a bus full of people stopped behind him. The bus driver honked loudly, but Dad didn't stop hacking away at the bureau. He kicked the drawers and broke off the sides.

People were hanging out the bus door to see what was going on. The bus driver honked again, and then reached for his cell phone.

"Dad, we're blocking the bus stop," said Lukas, pulling at Dad's sleeve. "We'd better leave."

"Just a minute," said Dad, still whacking away with the car jack. He flung the broken pieces of the bureau behind the bushes. Lukas saw him bend over, pick up a small red box, and stick it into his jacket pocket. He waved at the bus and got back into the car just as the police arrived. The people from the bus nosily gathered around Dad's car.

One of the police officers pushed them aside and said, "This is illegal dumping!"

"That deserves a ticket and a fine," said the other police officer.

Dad stood there befuddled and speechless. It was all a mystery to Lukas. If he had known what Dad's strange behavior was all about, he would have defended him. But he didn't have a chance because the first officer said to the other, "It's Christmas, let's forget about the ticket."

The second officer nodded, and said, "Okay, but there has to be a fine. We can't let him entirely off the hook."

With Lukas's help, Dad put what was left of the bureau back into his trunk. It fit easier than before, now that it was smashed to pieces. After the bus had driven off, one of the police officers climbed into the car with Dad and Lukas. The other officer followed them in the police car.

It was a good distance to the trash dump and, since it had just closed, Dad had to pay a surcharge because it was after hours. Then, he had to pay a hefty fee for disposing of the broken bureau. After that, Dad and Lukas had to pay a visit to the police station. Here, too, Dad had to pull out his wallet and pay. He received a lengthy sermon about dumping and creating a public nuisance. Finally they could go.

Once outside, Lukas still wanted to know why Dad wanted that old bureau so badly and why he had smashed it to bits. "I'll tell you later," said Dad.

Lukas was horrified by what Dad had done. First, there was the reckless chase. Then, there was the haggling over the bureau—only to destroy it afterward. And then, there was the part about the police. The strangest thing about all of this was that Dad didn't seem particularly upset.

"Don't make such a face," he said as they continued driving. "Nothing else can happen to us tonight!"

Unfortunately, something else did happen. The engine began to sputter and then it died. They were out of gas.

"Could you finally tell me what this is all about?" griped Lukas, as they hiked along the road with the empty gas can.

The closest gas station was pretty far away so Dad had plenty of time to explain everything to Lukas. "An awful story indeed. But it can't get any worse now," said Dad.

That's what he thought! After Dad had filled the can, he remembered that he didn't have any money. He swore that he would come back first thing tomorrow to pay, but the attendant would have none of it. Just before they were sent away with an empty gas can, Lukas remem-

bered the money Aunt Marie had given him.

Meanwhile, Mom was getting very worried. She had no idea why Dad and Lukas had disappeared after returning from Aunt Marie's. She sat by the window and waited. The candles had burned down, the tea was cold, and there weren't many cookies left when they finally walked in.

"What was the matter? Where were you?" she asked angrily.

Dad was so exhausted that he couldn't think of a suitable excuse. Since it was almost Christmas anyway, he decided to go with the truth and told Mom the whole story. Then, he pulled the tiny box from Aunt Marie from his pocket and gave it to her. Mom was speechless. She held the beautiful old brooch in one hand and brushed tears from her eyes with the other.

After she composed herself, she said, "Tomorrow, I am going to visit Aunt Marie and will ask her to celebrate Christmas with us. Is that okay with you?"

Dad gave Mom a hug, while Lukas devoured the rest of the cookies.

Barbara Dieck
SARAH'S SECRET SANTA

Scene: Schoolyard of the Edgar School, recess, the day before Christmas vacation. A group of girls and boys are standing together talking about the upcoming fifth period.
Agenda: Class Christmas party
Special Emphasis: Secret Santas

"Secret Santas?" asked a ninth grader. "Sounds stupid."

Good-natured Alexandra tried to explain it to him. "It's not stupid, it's really neat! We all wrote our names on a slip of paper and put them in Mr. Branson's hat. Then, we each drew a name from the hat. We're the Secret Santa for the person whose name we drew. Get it?"

"Like I said, stupid."

Tobias tried to help his classmate. "So if, for example, I drew Alex's name, then I'm her Secret Santa and I have to get her a present. And I have to write a poem so that people can try and guess who the gift is for. Got it?"

"That's totally infantile!" the boy said.

Tobias waved him off angrily.

"He's just jealous," said Yvonne. "I wish I knew who drew my name . . ."

"I know who my Santa is," insisted Nina. "I already know what my present is, too."

As usual, some students couldn't keep their mouths shut. Others gave themselves away with glances or overly secretive behaviors. Even Sarah was fairly sure about her Secret Santa's identity.

"Your Secret Santa is the Russian girl, isn't it?" asked Manuela softly. She peeked over at the new girl sitting on a bench. She wore shabby jeans, an old-fashioned sweater, and a lace bow in her hair. Another Russian girl from the sixth grade class sat next to her.

Sarah nodded. Ever since the name drawing, she had noticed the new girl looking at her, turning red each time their eyes met.

Manuela patted Sarah's arm. "Too bad—it doesn't look like you'll get anything you'll want."

"I think it's dumb that we aren't allowed to spend more than the limit Mr. Branson set," complained Neil. "What can you get for that amount?"

Anne planted her hands on her hips and mimicked their teachers, "Just remember, money isn't everything. You'll think of something. Make something yourselves. Let it come from your heart."

"Help!" cried Jan, and most of the students laughed. The new girl looked over and smiled shyly.

"I don't want a gift from the heart," said Nicole. "I want a new lip gloss from the store."

"There's something from the jewelry store in my gift box," revealed Catherine.

Something nice from a jewelry store wouldn't be bad, thought Sarah, but she wasn't too optimistic. The new girl probably didn't even get an allowance. Sarah had never seen her buy anything from the school store.

"If that Russian girl had drawn my name, I would have complained," said Sascha. "She has no money for a present. All her clothes are from the thrift store."

"Shut up!" hissed Ben. "She can hear you!"

"So what? Everyone knows her mother is a cleaning lady. She scrubs other people's toilets."

Shocked, Sarah looked over at the bench. Two dark eyes stared back.

"Shut up!" shouted Catherine. Ben lunged at Sascha, and several students chanted.

The new girl bent over toward her cheap sneakers and fingered the laces, while the girl next to her put her arm on her shoulders and comforted her.

"I'll bet Sarah gets a crocheted potholder or something like that," said Anne. "Something you could put straight in the garbage."

Sarah had heard enough. "I don't care what I get! Secret Santas are stupid anyway." The bell rang.

A group of students had decorated the room during recess. Candles and pine boughs were on the tables. Instead of his briefcase, Mr. Branson carried in the basket of presents. The new girl squeezed through the doorway behind him and hurried to her seat. Sarah tried to catch her eye, but the girl never looked up.

The door opened again. Max pulled Daniela behind him. She could hardly control her giggles. He was wearing a red bathrobe and beard, and she was dressed up as an elf. The class whooped and jeered.

"Behave yourselves," warned Mr. Branson, getting out his guitar. Despite loud protests, he insisted on making them sing several Christmas songs and take turns reciting poems. His students were still not paying attention.

"I bought a candle," whispered Mona, who sat on Sarah's left. "It's star-shaped, with glitter on it."

Yvonne, who had just finished her rhyme during the singing, brought her gift to the front of the room. It was something in a long, narrow tube. She dropped it in the basket.

"I'll bet that's a poster,"

said Catherine. "Probably Brad Pitt."

Mr. Branson finally put down his guitar. Santa Claus Max read the first Secret Santa poem:

I'm for a girl who likes to look the best.
She enjoys fine jewels
and is always well dressed.

That was an easy one to guess. Everyone agreed it was for Alexandra. The elf handed her a tiny box, and she unwrapped a pair of silvery earrings.

Neil was next. The poem about him was cheesy, but he liked his gift of sports pictures.

Sarah's heart beat a little faster as Max reached for the box she had wrapped for Thomas.

He is tall, pretty thin,
and ping pong is his game.
This present's for him,
if you can guess his name.

Once again, the recipient was quickly identified, and he was excited about the ping pong balls.

The game continued. Some of the gifts and poems proved that the Secret Santas had put some thought into their choices. But others . . .

"Oh, well. Better luck next year."

A little disappointed, Catherine put down the plastic ruler and protractor set.

When the new girl got her present, no one could guess who it was for. It was wrapped in wrinkled paper and held together with a rubber band. Max tried in vain to read the scribbles on the tag, until Harry called out, "It's for the Russian!"

The new girl turned pale and sank even deeper into her chair.

"Harry, you mean, it's for Elena, don't you? Your classmate's name is Elena," said Mr. Branson.

Shyly, she accepted the gift, and slowly unwrapped it. A package of chocolate bars emerged. "Thank you," said Elena softly.

A number of students found something they liked in their presents, but not all of them were happy.

"Nuts. Whoopee," whined Anne. "Anyone want to trade?"

John misjudged his friend's taste, too. "Yuck, no way will I eat that!" Dennis tossed a marzipan cookie across the table, causing the candle to flicker.

Finally, it was Sarah's turn.

"It doesn't say anything on here," Max held up the gift tag, grinning. "But, it's easy to tell whose picture this is."

"Sarah! It's Sarah. That's really well drawn!"

A smile flashed across Elena's face and, as Sarah smiled at her, her face turned beet red. Her classmates looked on as Sarah opened the wrapping paper and held a round metal container in her hand.

"Open it!" urged Catherine. No sooner was the lid unscrewed, than . . .

"Mmmm . . . what is that delicious smell? It's making my mouth water!" Mona sniffed enthusiastically at the carefully stacked little cakes. They smelled of spices, nuts, and candied fruits.

Sarah carefully took one out and took a tiny bite. When she realized that Elena was watching her, she shoved the rest into her mouth and smacked her lips.

"Yummy!" Sarah laughed to her Secret Santa. "This is the most delicious thing I have ever tasted!" This time, Elena did not lower her gaze. The timid smile grew, spreading from ear to ear.

Sarah let Catherine try a bite of one of her cakes, but only Catherine and no one else.

"What do you think? Should we ask Elena if she'd like to come with us to the Christmas party at my house?"

"Mmmm, hmm!" Catherine nodded with her mouth full. "Why not?"

Gesine Schulz
THE VERY BEST TREE

"Why can't I be an angel?" Jewel felt her face turning red. Her bottom lip stuck out. It was so unfair!

"Because we already have enough angels, Jewel. I've already explained that to you." Mrs. Mayer glanced up from her list.

Jewel hung her head.

"And remember," said the teacher, "you'll have almost two minutes on the stage all by yourself. It's like a solo, Jewel. No one else has that."

No, no one else in the play would have to stand on the stage for two minutes doing nothing at all except be a fir tree in the forest, symbolizing the passage of time. The five angels got to wear glittery robes, stars in their hair, and little wings on their backs.

"Well, Jewel? Make up your mind. Can I sign you up as the tree?"

Jewel did not look up. She nodded—if that was the only way to be in the Christmas play.

"It's so unfair," said Jewel as she set the table with her mother that evening. "I really wanted to be an angel. And Grandma had offered to sew my costume out of this white, glittery fabric."

"Oh, Jewel, dear, I'm sorry that you're so disappointed."

Jewel stuck out her lower lip.

"What part does Barbara have?"

"She's singing in the choir. I practiced the song with her today while we were roller-skating. Tomorrow, we'll go ice-skating. I want to see if I can do a pirouette on the ice, too."

"You two are always on the go. I get tired just thinking about all that exercise! Please go down and tell Dad that dinner is ready."

Dad would have to help her build her tree. "We'll have to make it out of cardboard in the shape of a Christmas tree," Jewel explained to him. "I'll need it to have handles on the back, so I can hold it. I can paint it green myself."

Then all she would need were brown shoes and stockings. She didn't even need make-up, since her face wouldn't be visible.

Everyone was talking about their costumes. Even the choir was making silvery tinsel wigs. Jewel spray-painted her cardboard tree green. Then she gave it a kick.

She visited her grandma in the nursing home. "It's a really stupid role, if you can even call it a role," Jewel complained, as she helped herself to another Christmas cookie.

"Hmm," said Grandma, "I think you should speak to Mr. Groner. He lives at the end of the hall."

"The one with the mustache?"

"That's right. He used to be an actor. Maybe he could give you some advice."

Mr. Groner visited Grandma at tea-time. He drank three cups of tea while Jewel told her story. "Tell me, Jewel, is it an old tree?"

"I don't know."

"Is it tall or short? Did it grow straight or crooked? Are there birds' nests among its branches?"

"Who cares? Does it really matter?"

Mr. Groner laughed and held up his hand. "Of course it does. If you want to be good, you have to feel the part. It doesn't matter whether you play an angel, a donkey, or a tree. You have to know everything about it. You have to feel what it feels. You have to *be* this tree, Jewel. And no matter how small your part is, always try to be the best you can be. That is the secret. You understand?"

Jewel nodded. She thought she knew what he meant. At least she had a vague idea.

"Once when I had to prepare for a small role as a waiter, I sat in a café for days observing the waiters there. I watched them until I knew exactly what my own waiter would be like, right down to the number of corns on his feet."

"Thank you, Mr. Groner," said Jewel. TMI, she thought to herself. Too Much Information.

Jewel had wanted to spend the night in the forest, but her parents had been against that. But they did allow her to spend two hours in the neighbors' garden after nightfall—way back in a corner where three fir trees grew. The wind rustled through the branches, making them sway gently. The trees groaned. Dry twigs crackled. Her face became cold. The wind picked up. It was like a dance to the wind's music. Jewel got an idea, and when she presented it to Mrs. Mayer, she didn't object.

Dad started to design a new costume. "We'll make a floor-length wire frame that rests on your shoulders and ends in a point over your head. Then, you'll need a pair of movable branches, connected to your fingers with strings. When you wiggle your fingers, you'll move the branches." Grandma sewed pieces of artificial greens onto the frame. Mom put make-up on her face, which peered out of the greens. She made Jewel a green face with red cheeks and a red button nose.

The first act ended. Mrs. Mayer gave Jewel her cue. Jewel pushed off on her roller skates. The audience looked up to see a small, chubby fir tree glide out onto the stage and stop, motionless. It slowly got dark. A wind picked up, rustling softly, and then more loudly. The tree's branches began to move up and down, in time with the wind. They heard the sounds of a storm, with whistling and howling. The tree swayed back and forth. It groaned. The wind died down. It became still, just as the moon was rising.

In the distance, a bell began to chime. One, two . . . It started to snow. Three, four . . . The snow fell more thickly. Five, six . . . The tree was almost white, and glittered in the moonlight. Seven, eight . . . More snow fell. Nine, ten, eleven, twelve. At last, the snow stopped. The stage was empty.

"Excellent," said Mrs. Mayer to Jewel backstage. "Bravo." The fir tree did a pirouette, just for herself. Five angels stomped past as they went onstage. Jewel hardly noticed them. Next year she wanted to be a fir tree again.

Carolin Philipps

GRANNY.COM

Everyone in his class had a grandma, except Michael. Michael would have loved having a grandma, especially at Christmastime. His friend Mark had asked his parents for a PlayStation, and when they said no, his grandma said yes!

Michael had plenty of his own wishes, ones he knew his parents would not grant. But, unlike Mark, he had no grandma to fulfill them. He thought this was pretty unfair.

"Maybe you could rent one!" Mark suggested helpfully. "My father says you can rent anything these days."

But Michael didn't believe that you could rent a grandma.

Time was precious. Christmas was only eight weeks away, and there was no grandma in sight.

"Advertise on the Internet," suggested Mark.

"You're crazy!" said Michael. "Who'd see an ad like that? Have you ever heard of any grandmas surfing the web?"

Mark shook his head. His grandma liked to knit, and she was a good artist. And when it came to baking, she was a better than the one in town.

But, she wasn't interested in computers.

Michael had almost resigned himself to the fact that he just wouldn't find himself a grandma in time for Christmas. Then, something odd happened. Late that evening he heard his parents talking loudly.

"The doctor said it wasn't serious. She'll be able to get back up in two days. It was just some mild circulatory trouble—nothing more." His father sounded a little irritated.

"Perhaps you should visit her—or at least call?"

"What for? If she wanted to see me, she could have called me years ago." Michael could tell that his father didn't want to talk about it.

"Maybe she was waiting for you to call her. She's your mother, after all."

Michael couldn't believe his ears. He had a grandma!

No one had ever told him about her. How could they keep a secret like this from him? He was ready to run straight to the kitchen to confront them. But then again . . . If his father hadn't talked to her in years, he wasn't likely to contact her now just because Michael wanted a grandma.

No, he would have to take matters into his own hands.

If she was Father's mother, then she must have the same last name: Brenner. Maybe she had a telephone. There were three Brenners in the phone book. One was his father, Harold. Then there was a Peter and a Marta.

He anxiously dialed the number for Marta Brenner.

"Do you have a son named Harold?" he asked as soon as she answered.

"Why, yes, I do. Is he all right?" The voice sounded worried.

"Oh, yes!" said Michael. "Everything's fine. He said to say hello. And he hopes you feel better soon."

"Why?"

Michael hung up. Her address was listed next to her name: 15 King Street. After school the next day, he took a bus there. As he stood there, wondering what to do next, the door opened and a woman came out. That had to be her!

He followed her to the senior center and watched her through the window. A young man was showing her how to send e-mail. "Martha_Brenner@seniorcenter.com," she muttered to herself as she typed out the letters. "And now I can send letters? Without stamps?"

The young man nodded.

"But I don't know anyone who has an e-mail address."

"Practice first!" advised the young man. "The rest will take care of itself."

He had no idea how right he was. Michael was already on his way home to his computer.

"Dear Grandma," he wrote, "you don't know me, but I've seen you. Won't you please write to me? Sincerely, your grandson Michael."

Apparently, his grandma was still practicing at the center. In any case, her response arrived a few minutes later. "Hi, Michael! Nice to meet you!"

That was the beginning of their e-mail friendship. Many e-mails went back and forth each day. He wrote to her about his parents and about school. She wrote that she would like to meet him.

"Why don't I know you?" Michael wanted to know.

His grandma replied that many years ago, she'd had an argument with Michael's father. It was so serious that neither one wanted to speak with the other anymore. "Unfortunately, a stubborn streak runs in the family," she wrote.

Michael decided it was time to break with family tradition and just go visit her, and so began his best holiday season ever. His grandma did not knit or bake, but she knew the names of all the Blue Devils hockey players.

"Your grandma goes to hockey games?" asked Mark, surprised and a little jealous.

Michael nodded proudly. "She has tickets for tomorrow."

He and his grandma visited all of the Christmas markets in the city. They also went ice-skating together. His grandma wasn't fast, but she was steady on her skates.

"So, did you give her your wish list yet?" Mark wanted to know.

Michael shook his head. He had forgotten all about why he had started searching for a grandma in the first place.

"Does she at least have money?" asked Mark.

Michael shrugged his shoulders. "I have no idea. But she has time. Time for me."

Mark looked at him thoughtfully.

Just before Christmas, Michael sprained his ankle during gym class. He e-mailed her and told her about his accident. That night, he sat at his computer and read her reply. She was very concerned.

"For Christmas," she wrote, "I wish that we could all be together."

Just then, the phone rang. His father poked his head through the door. "It's Mark. He wants to talk to you."

When Michael came back to his desk, his computer had been turned off. "Why did you turn it off?" he called out to his father.

Michael didn't like it when his parents touched his computer. His father sat in front of the television, staring blankly at the screen.

"Dad?" No answer.

Over the next few days, his father seemed absent-minded. And then, three days before Christmas, his father came into his room, looking a bit embarrassed. Michael looked at him questioningly.

"When you write to your grandma, tell her that we'll both go visit her tomorrow. It will be an early Christmas present."

Michael was sure that she was probably sitting at her computer and that she'd received his message. After all, this was the time of day when she always sent her e-mails. Still, it took a long time for the answer to arrive. When it did, it was very short: "Tell your father I said Merry Christmas."

Annette Herzog
MY STUPID SISTER HANNAH

Anyone who doesn't have a big sister like I do has no idea how exhausting it can be. This is especially true if said sister is in the eighth grade and is unhappily in love. And on top of that, if it's December.

Last year, she spoiled the entire Advent season for me with her pitiful puppy dog eyes. Instead of going ice-skating as she usually did, she lay on her bed, staring into space, listening to mournful music. She wouldn't listen to anything I tried to tell her.

Of course, my friend Anna and I soon discovered what this was all about. It wasn't hard to figure out when Hannah's gaze followed Robert all over the schoolyard at recess. Robert was in the ninth grade, wore pants whose waist seemed to hang down to his knees, and had dark, dreamy eyes. I had to agree, he was good-looking. But she hung around the house with a sad face and completely ruined my usual joyful anticipation of Christmas. And he'd never even called her—my stupid sister Hannah hadn't even talked to him. When she told me this I nearly had a fit!

"That can't be!" I roared, throwing myself onto the bed. "Just go up to him and say hello!"

"I can't just go up and start talking to him. He'll think I'm the village idiot. What if I can't think of anything to say after hello? What if he laughs at me? What if he doesn't like me?"

"If you won't talk to him then I will!" I said. "I'm not scared!"

"Don't you dare!" cried Hannah as she jumped off the bed. "I'll kill you!"

"I bet you don't even know his last name, do you?" I asked.

"I do so, it's Beckerman," replied Hannah, making a face at me.

"Hannah Beckerman!" I said, laughing. I ran from her room, the pillow she threw just missing my head. She had no sense of humor anymore.

"Don't you dare talk to him!" she called after me.

The situation didn't improve. The second Sunday of Advent came,

and the third, and then I had only seven un-opened doors left on my Advent calendar. Hannah hadn't opened more than the first two. It had snowed, and you couldn't pass the park without being bombarded with snow-balls. The hill saw lots of sledding activity and the slide on the playground seemed slicker than ever. In previous years, Hannah and I had been there all the time. This year, I only succeeded in luring her out once.

"Robert is out sledding!" I called, and Hannah actually sprang off her bed.

"Really? Are you telling the truth?" She stormed over to her window and saw that he actually was there.

"I'm hurt, would I lie to you?" I asked.

Of course Hannah had to go sledding right away. She didn't even have time to search for her mittens. We squeezed ourselves onto the sled, which had gotten too small for the two of us. But she was too embarrassed to go alone. "He might think I'm following him," she said. Lame-o, I thought to myself.

That's when it happened. After all, someone had to do something!

"We're going to run into him!" I cried. We were flying down the slope at top speed and I had spotted Robert standing at the bottom of the hill. "Then he will have to say something to you!"

"Stop it!" Hannah screamed in my ear. "Don't!"

I shoved my left leg into the snow in order to steer our sled in Robert's direction. Somehow Hannah shoved in the other direction. In any case we started spinning and flew ungracefully sideways down the hill landing almost directly next to Robert. He looked at my sister and grinned, the way you grin when someone falls off their sled. Nonetheless, I did notice that he was blushing at the same time.

We went home immediately. Hannah didn't fume the way I had expected her to. Instead, she sat silently wiping the tears from her face, and that was much, much worse. I truly felt sorry for her. Still the more I thought about Robert and how his face had turned red, the more I was sure that there was hope. I just had to give them a little push.

That evening, I visited my friend Anna. She was all for action when she heard what I had in mind.

"On the last day of school before Christmas vacation?" Anna giggled. "December 22."

The day arrived and everything was set. Anna had gotten Robert's class schedule and I already knew Hannah's. They both had classes during sixth period. It couldn't have worked out better. Anna and I got out of school after fifth period. We had a whole hour to put my plan into action.

We rushed to my house after the bell rang. I yanked a bag out of my closet. Yesterday, I had filled it with everything we would need: Hannah's fur hat with earflaps, her black-and-white jacket, her favorite pink patterned scarf, and a sign that read: IN LOVE WITH ROBERT.

"Don't you think she might kill you?" Anna asked, a little concerned, as we ran all the way to Robert's house. He lived directly on the street that led from school to my house.

"I don't care," I said, although I had to admit that I was a little nervous. But I would not give up now. We came to a stop in front of Robert's house.

"I'll ring the bell and see if anyone is home," I said, hoping no one would spoil my plan by answering the door. We were in luck—no answer! "You make the stomach, I'll make the head."

Like two madmen we rolled the balls of snow through the yard. Ten minutes later, a perfect snowman, round and indestructible, sat next to Robert's gate.

"It's a little too fat to be Hannah," said Anna as she tried to slim the snowman down while I pressed the brown button eyes into its face.

"It doesn't matter." I pulled Hannah's hat onto the snowman's head, buttoned Hannah's jacket around it, and tossed on the pink scarf. Finally I jammed the sign into the front of my snow-sister's body. IN LOVE WITH ROBERT. If this didn't work, nothing would!

We ran through Robert's yard and hid behind a wooden shed.

We didn't have to wait long. The bell had rung, and we could already hear the first students on their way home from school. It was Christmas vacation! I peeked cautiously around the corner of the shed.

"Robert's coming!" I whispered.

Anna held her hand to her mouth to stiffle her giggles.

My heart hammered so loudly I was sure Anna could hear it. What if my plan failed? Robert was the first one to arrive. He stood speechless in front of his gate. I could see the others making their way casually in groups. My sister was in front with one of her friends. When she saw the snowman in Robert's yard, she stopped dead in her tracks.

"That's my scarf!" she cried, lunging toward the snowman. "And my hat, AND my jacket! Who did this?" Bewildered she stared at Robert. "Did you put that sign there?"

I saw Robert step aside in shock. Anna had crawled up next to me. She stared around the corner of the shed, spellbound.

In the meantime, the other students had stopped in front of Robert's house, grinning. Hannah tore the sign from the snowman's stomach and started to smack Robert with it. Suddenly we both had to giggle. As she tried to smack Robert on the head with the cardboard sign, he looked for a way to escape, unable to defend himself. It was too funny. I had always known not to play tricks on my sister! When Anna starts to laugh there is no stopping her. She laughed so loudly that Hannah turned around. You could see the light-bulb go off in her head. "Ohhhhhh, you two . . ." She dropped the sign and lunged for us, but we were ready for her. She never had a chance against the barrage of snow-balls that came flying her way. In the meantime, Robert caught on, too. He hurried to my sister's aid. I hadn't had such a won-derful snowball fight in a long time! Soon the other students had all dropped their schoolbooks and Anna and I were surround-ed. Our only option—run for our lives! Unfortunate-ly, our gales of laughter made it difficult to even walk, let alone flee!

"I'll help you," cried Hannah, and suddenly she was on our side. She, too, was giggling happily. "Let's get him!" Try as she might though, her snowballs never hit their intended target. That is why she ran directly toward Robert, a gigantic snowball balanced in her hands. But he was quicker. Grinning he took the snowball from her hands and rubbed her face with it. Christmas was saved!

Anna and I grinned at each other with satisfaction, and then we left. Sensing that the action had ended, the others slipped quietly away as well.

We didn't need to build a snowman this year. Robert is practically a fixture in our house, and our homemade sign hangs on Hannah's bedroom door.

Now it's my turn to wait for that last school day before Christmas break, because this year, I'm the one who fell in love.

I'm half hoping—and half fearing—that a snowman will appear in front of Steven's door on my way home.

Evelyne Stein-Fischer
WHAT A PRESENT!

All the other children will get presents for Christmas. But I'm getting a sister. A tiny, wrinkly, stinky baby. As if I weren't enough for my parents!

I saw a newborn baby at my aunt's house. I thought it looked a lot like the baby orangutan at the zoo. I was glad my parents weren't having anymore babies.

And then, Wham! It happened. At first, my parents kept it a secret. When they told me about it, with sparkling eyes and beaming smiles, Christmas was still far away.

And now, this dumb Sister No-name is coming. Mom is in the hospital because she thought the baby was on its way today. The doctor decided that she should stay there in case of complications and because the stress of preparing for Christmas at home wouldn't be good for her. Meanwhile, I'm the one who's stressed!

What ten-year-old wants an unfamiliar, screaming dwarf in their room? Great present, right? On top of that, I finally got my own television last year. Now its' out with the TV and in with the baby. Mom claimed it's because of the noise and harmful rays. Just fabulous!

Tomorrow, I'll probably be sitting in front of the Christmas tree all by myself, while Dad is at the hospital with Mom. He absolutely wants to be there for the birth. They don't want me there anyway.

"If the baby arrives tomorrow, I'll take you to Aunt Miriam's house," Dad announced from the living room. She's the one with the baby orangutan. It is starting to look pretty human lately, but it is noisy and makes dirty diapers. At least it was smart enough not to turn the whole family upside down by choosing to come in December.

Dad is already completely mixed up. Instead of it being full of pre-Christmas cheer, this December is one of "not nows." No matter what I ask Dad, his answer is "not now!"

Today he came home from work at lunchtime. Ever since, he's been puttering around, testing the crib rails as if my baby sister could secretly escape before she has even arrived. He is so hysterical even though Mom's the one having the baby.

Silly me—with lots of effort, I learned a really long, beautiful poem for Mom by heart. That was a real achievement for me because I can't stand poems. But Mom writes them herself, and so I thought up this surprise for her for Christmas. And she would have been surprised.

The poem has seven stanzas. I wrote the last two myself and printed out the whole thing on the computer with pretty decorations. I used colorful borders, Christmas symbols, and a heart—because after all, she is my mom.

Except soon she won't just be my mom anymore. She'll also be mom of dumb Sister No-name.

It's snowing outside, heavy, huge flakes that don't melt right away after landing.

We'll see how Dad reacts when I ask him if he wants to build a snowman with me. We haven't done that in a long time because it hasn't snowed enough in a long time. If Dad says "not now" again, I'll go over to Oliver's. At his house, it has already smelled like Christmas for days. They have set up their tree and his mother has been baking tons of cookies. She's even baked vanilla crescents. I really like those because they melt on your tongue like the snowflakes outside. Only they are sweet, vanilla flavored, and nutty.

At our house, the oven is cold and there are no cookies waiting for me. Did my parents even remember to buy me presents? Didn't Mom say, just one week ago, "A child who is born around Christmas is the biggest and most beautiful gift in the world!"

Did that count for me, too, and am I seriously only getting that Sister No-name? In any case, it's true for Dad. He had nodded to Mom and looked very happy. He looked even happier than when his soccer team had won 4–3 in the eighty-eighth minute of the game.

I have tried to look forward to this. Honestly, I have. But I just can't do it. Mom noticed this as always and stroked my head reassuringly. "You will always be our Andrew! Our big Andrew!"

And here, I wanted to be a little Andrew, a very little one. I wanted to be without an intruder in the family. Maybe everything would still turn out okay.

Dad was talking to Mom

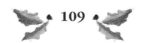

on the telephone. "And what did the doctor say to that? I see. And how long has this been going on? Do you think? Well, I don't know. If I were you, I'd . . ."

It seemed that Mom had cut him off, because Dad just listened to her for a while without saying anything. I can just imagine how she answered: I know very well what I have to do. Stop seeing everything so negatively. You're not helping me by doing that. Don't worry about it. That's what she always says, and Dad continues worrying about whatever IT is. I can tell by his face when he hangs up the phone.

"Is something going on?" I ask.

"Mom doesn't sound good. She is in a lot of pain. And you know we practiced the right kind of breathing together in the prenatal class."

I didn't like that either, when Dad went with Mom to that silly class. Like he thought he was having the baby. Mom explained to me that it's very important for a mother to have the father's support. If he knows what to expect, he can help Mom to relax at the right time.

And who was there to help me? I am also under a great deal of stress.

"Maybe I'll go visit her again later," said Dad. "It's important to her."

Of course it is important to her. I understand that. I don't want Mom to be in pain. I am not important now. I understand that, too. It is Sister No-name's turn. For the first time, I wish that she'd hurry up and get here so that Mom isn't in pain. Maybe it will happen today. For all I care, we can then celebrate Christmas together next year. Maybe she won't look like a newborn orangutan and will behave herself. As it is, babies usually sleep all the time anyway.

"Will you build a snowman with me, Dad?" He's not supposed to think about Melanie right now. That's what Sister No-name will be called. I want him to pay attention to me!

First, Dad ran his fingers through his hair. He was obviously wondering whether to drive over to Mom or to stay with me.

"Okay, fine!" he said suddenly. "Maybe this will distract me. Let's go into the yard. The snow is just right. But I'll take the cell phone along so that I can be reached."

My hands are freezing as we start to throw snowballs at each other. We have a wild time, as though everything were just as usual. The snowman grows taller, one layer at a time. Soon, there are three of us in the yard: me, Dad, and the snowman.

Suddenly Dad said, "You're going to love the gift we have for you!" I knew right away that this was a real present, one that had nothing to do with Sister No-name.

"It is fairly large," described Dad. He indicated the size with his hands, but I still couldn't guess what it was. I could only imagine it. My heart pounded.

Excited, I stroked the snowman's icy, bald head. He didn't have a hat or carrot nose. He was naked, with stone eyes.

"Look," said Dad suddenly. He bent down and rubbed his flattened hand over the big, round snow tummy. "It's almost like Mom's."

"It's much colder and there's nothing in it," I said, irritated. Dad glanced over at me. My comment gave him a scare, but I didn't know exactly why. I tried to smile, but didn't quite succeed.

"It was only a joke," I said, "a stupid one."

Dad stood up. Looking me straight in the eye, he took both of my hands. "That was no joke and it was also not stupid," he said softly and seriously. He was quiet for a while as he looked at me searchingly. "You are afraid. I am, too, but for different reasons."

"That all sounds very complicated. You're just looking on the negative side again, Dad." His good mood was gone. He was worried about Mom and about everything that could go wrong with the birth and the baby.

"Calm down, Dad. What does the stupid snowman have to do with Mom? She's not alone in the hospital. Besides, they know what they are doing. Babies are born there every day, happily screaming their little heads off. Tons of doctors and nurses are there. That hospital specializes in births!"

"I know." Dad wound his scarf more tightly around his neck. "Come, let's go inside. It's getting cold."

He checked to make sure the cell phone was actually turned on, even though it would only be thirty seconds before we were inside where the telephone is.

Dad sat on the couch with me. We talked about life, like two grown men. Dad said that life is a miracle and that every moment and every person is precious. "Even evil people?" I asked.

"They are not born evil," answered Dad. "I believe that all people are born good. Unfortunately, much can happen to them later, and that has an effect on them."

"Melanie will be good," I said suddenly.

"I'm sure," said Dad, "just like you!"

"And I will make sure that she stays good!"

"I knew I could depend on you!" Dad laughed.

I didn't know exactly what he meant by that. But I do know that I started to look forward—at least a little—to this Sister No-name who would belong to us, as of tomorrow.

Karla Schneider
THE SUBSTITUTES

Whatever was hidden behind the living room door had been a total mystery. It was that way since Grandma and Grandpa arrived, laden with huge bags that they immediately stashed in the living room.

No one thought to turn on the light in the bedroom. Right now, Annie would rather wait in the twilight anyway. There was some light from the kitchen shining through the glass door. Dad was standing in the kitchen with his apron on, making potato salad. Now and then, he snacked on tiny pickles. Annie and Noah only ate the little sausages; neither of them cared much for potato salad.

Noah, Annie's little brother, sat in his highchair, helping Dad by drumming on the corner of the table with a whisk. He was only two.

The door to the living room opened. What was visible through the crack was suspiciously shiny. Grandpa squeezed through and quickly closed the door behind him.

"Well, the Christmas tree is all set up," he said, satisfied. He noticed Annie and pointed his thumb mysteriously toward the living room. Whispering, he asked, "Do you know who arrived earlier? He's in there now. He brought a lot of stuff with him." Then Grandpa knocked on the door.

"Hello, Santa Claus, are you still there? Annie doesn't believe me."

In reply, there were three stomps from behind the door.

"You can hear for yourself," said Grandpa. "Shall I turn on the light?" Annie shook her head.

Grandpa went into the kitchen. "I managed to get the tree looking pretty good," he said to Dad.

Annie snuck out of the bedroom, past the open kitchen door. Dad and Grandpa were laughing about something and weren't paying attention. No one saw Annie hide herself in the hallway, in the corner next to the coat closet. When Santa Claus came out of the living room, he would have to walk past her. Then, Annie would pop out of her hiding place and grab him by his coat. Unfortunately, this plan hadn't worked last year because Santa was always in such a terrible hurry. Maybe they could finally talk to each other. Annie could also sing something for him. Grandma had met him once when she was a child. She still remembered it all in great detail.

Annie listened very carefully. It was strange that Santa Claus didn't say a word in the living room. She only heard Mom and Grandma. Since it was taking so long for him to come

out, Annie looked out the hallway window. She could see a little bit of the road and the garages across the street. Lonely footsteps along the road were coming closer. A big shadow scurried past the garages. The shadow was followed by the person to whom the shadow belonged. Annie couldn't believe what she saw!

The person who was down there on the street was wearing a long, green velvet coat. On his head was a tall, green velvet hat. The brim was made of pine branches instead of fur. Something was the matter with his beard. It was neither snow-white nor did it reach his chest. It was just around his chin. A sack dangled from his shoulder. But the sack was clearly empty.

Wait a minute, just who was inside the parlor? Grandpa wouldn't lie. Didn't the visitor stomp on the floor three times in answer to Grandpa's question?

Annie observed the Santa ringing the doorbell next door, where the Smiths lived. Didn't he know that they didn't have any children?

They must have set him straight immediately, because now he was on his way to the Hubbles's door. The Hubbles were away on a trip. They went "to catch some sun." At least that is what Mrs. Hubble told Mom. Before Santa Claus had a chance to ring her doorbell, Annie opened it in anticipation. But Santa stopped on the steps. He didn't seem to want to cross the threshold.

"Hello? Anyone home?" he called in a deep, resonant voice. He pressed the doorbell, even though the door was already open.

Grandpa rushed out of the kitchen. Mom and Grandma hurried to the door from the Christmasy room full of presents. "You are running early!" said Grandpa.

"Just a minute! Who is that," said Mom.

"Santa Claus," Annie whispered to Mom. Why didn't she recognize Santa? But no one seemed to hear her. Mom made no effort to invite the main character of the evening inside.

She said to the others, "There's no way that's Arnold Peters. This guy is almost six feet tall. And look at his beard. It looks like it's real. Arnold Peters doesn't even shave yet. Are you a substitute? Did something happen to Arnold?"

"I have no idea." Santa Claus cleared his throat self-consciously. "I was just going door-to-door. It's twenty dollars per appearance. I have my own sack."

"Too bad. We already have other arrangements," said Grandma. "If only we'd known sooner! You really have a gorgeous costume. The idea of using pine branches as your brim is very original. You should take a photo, Eric. Go get your camera."

Dad was still wearing his apron. He brought Santa a glass of eggnog. "We're sorry. Your colleague beat you to it. But why don't you have some eggnog in honor of the day?"

Ding! Dong! The doorbell rang again. Dreamily, Annie opened the door. She didn't know what to believe anymore. She was standing very close to Santa Claus. Yet oddly enough, he hadn't shown any interest in her whatsoever. Since she was a child, you would think he would pay some attention to her. She knew that Santas only come because of the children. In fact, no one seemed to see or hear her at all. Suddenly she felt sad. Something was wrong. Terribly wrong.

"Merry Christmas!" said someone through the open door. At first the voice was high pitched, and then it became deep and manly. It belonged to another Santa Claus.

He was much shorter than the first one. On his head was a red Santa hat that was just like Annie and Noah's. The thin threads of his white cotton beard were caught in his fur coat, revealing the cloth to which the cotton was attached. This Santa's fur coat reached down to his knees. It was cut wide, like a bell. Annie recognized that coat. Old Mrs. Peters wore it on extremely cold days.

"Ah, there he is. That's the right one," called Mom. "I'll take his sack from him."

Without a word, the new Santa handed her his empty sack. He shoved his hands into his coat pockets and leaned against the wall.

Mom and Grandma disappeared into the living room together. They took the sack in with them. Annie realized that neither adults nor Santas saw her standing there.

"Wait—don't go! I want to take a picture," called Dad, waving at the green Santa Claus. He ran to get his camera.

Tears welled up in Annie's eyes. They came suddenly. She tried to catch them with her tongue, since it wasn't right to blubber at Christmas, but her tongue was too short.

She felt a hand on her head. The hand lifted her chin. It was the hand of the Santa with the gray stubble beard and the crown of pines.

"Would you believe," he said, so softly that only Annie could hear, "the real Santa came 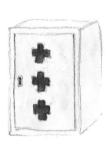 down with a bad case of conjunctivitis just before Christmas. He accidentally looked straight at the Northern Lights without wearing any eye protection. Now he's lying in bed, with chamomile compresses on his eyes every fifteen minutes. His vision is all foggy, and it's expected to remain like that for another week. He certainly was in no condition to drive that sleigh! That's why substitute Santas were dispatched this year. And since we didn't have time to work out the schedules properly, things are a little confused. He'll come again in person next year. Shall I give him a message from you?"

"Yes, please," said Annie. She swallowed and smiled. So that was what was going on! What message should she give the poor, sick Santa? She knew what! She ran to the bathroom and opened the medicine cabinet, which was normally strictly forbidden.

"Here, give him this," she said conspiratorially.

"Eye drops," the substitute Santa read, holding the tiny vial close to his eyes.

"They always helped Dad," said Annie. "Please tell him to get well soon. And also tell him, that if he had come, I would have sung "Santa Claus Is Coming to Town" for him. I'll wait until next year."

"Take your places, everyone!" Dad was ready with his camera. Grandpa appeared, carrying Noah.

"This will be our documentation of the Night of the Santa Substitutes!" Dad glowed with enthusiasm and held the camera to his eye. "Santa Clauses in the middle. Everyone get a little closer, please." Annie tried to catch the nice substitute's eye. He winked at her. Dad took several pictures, moving people and Santas all around.

"Will this take much longer?" asked the substitute who came last. "Because . . . well, we are planning to eat at seven. And if I'm supposed to hand out the presents . . ."

"Soon, Arnold, soon," said Dad. "We'll be done here in a minute. Just one more picture: you two together with the kids. Will you hold Noah?"

The Santa named Arnold Peters knew nothing about children. Annie could see that right away. Just look at how he tried to deal with her wiggly brother! Meanwhile, Noah was trying desperately to pull off Santa's red hat. He probably thought it was his own.

"Listen, little one! Stop that! Move your hand! Hey, hey, easy on the beard!" Arnold Peters struggled to defend himself against Noah. Annie could have told him he had no chance. Noah only ever let go when he'd gotten what he wanted.

"My goodness! He's disgracing our whole profession," said Annie's Santa under his breath, shaking his head over his colleague's behavior.

Annie giggled. "What is your name?" It's funny how Santas have names like ordinary people.

"Actually, we're not allowed to reveal that. But, since it's you: my name is Herbert Bloom."

"And the real, true Santa Claus? What is his name?"

"Shhh," said Herbert Bloom, putting a finger to his lips. "No one is allowed to ask that. It must remain a secret. Even I don't know it."

Annie nodded. She thought it was much better that way, anyway.

Dad gave Herbert Bloom some money and shook his hand good-bye. Before he left, he gave Annie a secret smile. He patted his coat pocket, where he'd put the eye drops.

Then he was gone. Annie turned around and saw that the Christmasy parlor was wide open. Noah had finally managed to snatch Arnold's red hat. The beard, it seemed, had also come off during the battle. The Santa substitute rubbed his chubby red cheeks.

"It's not my fault," he griped. "Besides, I have to go home soon."

Annie was happy that Santa would soon have the eye drops, so he'd be better in time for next Christmas!

Doris Meißner-Johannknecht
THE TWENTY-FOURTH, CHRISTMAS EVE

SCENE 1
4:00 p.m. / Inside the house

"Silent Night" had been droning from every radio station all day long.
Snow was softly falling—it had been all day long. But not on the radio. No.
Seriously.
Right outside the door.
A White Christmas! I'd never had one of those before in my life.
It was totally nice.
This twenty-fourth of December.

And the best is still to come.
The evening. The one they call the holy one.
But that doesn't start until eight. Until then—chaos reigns.
Just like now.
My mother was in a rage, flipping out. She was completely beside herself again.
Same thing, different year.
Yes, the Christmas stress was back again!
And every year, the reasons for her fits changed.
Today, there were four reasons.

Reason Number One:
At eleven o'clock, Dad finally bought the Christmas tree.
Just like every year, he waited until the best ones were already gone. Until only the scrappy looking ones remain.
Yes, but then they are so much less expensive. They practically give them away.
Dad thinks it's great. Mom doesn't.
Today at eleven, he finally dragged in the tree.
An absolute bargain. But, it had three braches at the very top.
That's when Mom threw her first fit.
Totally uncalled for, really. It was pretty exceptional, that tree. Three tops!
I even made two more stars for the two extra tops. It looked awesome.
My mother flew into a rage anyway.

Reason Number Two:
At one o'clock, Dad finally set up the manger. Old family heirloom. Hand-carved. Quite valuable.
Yes, and Dad must have dug in too vigorously. In any case, Mary suddenly had only one arm. And we had no glue in the house.

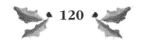

Reason Number Three:

Happened at three o'clock. And that was one reason too many.

This time my mother didn't fly into a rage. She just sobbed.

Someone hadn't shut the door to the pantry properly.

And just as Mom went to take out the Christmas goose, she saw Anton the cat brush past her. The incarnate guilty conscience.

Mom assumed the worst.

And that is exactly what had happened. Anton the cat had devoured the best of the best. Raw.

The wonderfully tender goose breast from the organic farm.

Dad grinned.

I giggled.

Mom sobbed.

And Anton? He would remain out of sight for a while. He was full.

I retreated to my room to wrap presents for the relatives who would come to visit us tomorrow.

Reason Number Four:

Happened at four o'clock. The highlight of the day for the time being.

All of a sudden, without knocking, my mother appeared in my room. She saw me surrounded by paper and boxes and stuff and yelled: "Too much chaos on Christmas Eve, and I have to do all the work!"

I covered my ears. And said: "If you don't stop screaming, I'm leaving!"

But my mother didn't stop. She couldn't. She said: "Fine, then leave!"

And I left.

Pretty dumb, really.

SCENE 2
5:00 p.m. / In front of the house

So then there I was, outside. Without a scarf and without a jacket. Hoping, just a little, that my mother would come out and bring me back inside.

She didn't.

So I walked away. With a guilty conscience. Despite my anger. Pretty dumb. All of it.

Sometimes things are like that.

On Christmas Day following Christmas Eve, mother was going to have her five siblings over. Same as every year.

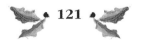

With their whole entourage. My aunts and uncles and cousins. About twenty people.

That's why she's been cooking and baking like mad for days.

Until she went nuts. On Christmas Eve.

SCENE 3
6:00 p.m. / At the market square

The wooden booths of the Christmas market were closed. No crowds pushing. No tasty aromas. Nothing.

No one was out and about.

Everything was covered under a white blanket of snow. Peaceful and nice. Christmasy somehow.

The cathedral bells rang for mass. Hordes of people crowded through the entrance. In their Sunday best. Hair freshly washed. Everyone looked festive.

No, not everyone.

Besides me, there was one other person who was walking around as lost as I was. And who also didn't look especially festive. On the contrary.

Pretty ragged. But also pretty colorful. Not just the clothing and the backpack. The hair, too.

It all looked like a rainbow somehow. Exciting and beautiful.

I approached cautiously. Hid behind a shop. A short distance still separated us.

It was a girl, a few years older than me. She was headed toward an older woman. Stretched out her hand. Smiled, said a few sentences.

The woman opened her purse, pulled out a wallet, and put a coin into the outstretched hand. The girl smiled again, spoke a little, and headed for a young man. He reached into his pocket, and so on, until no one else came around.

Organ music rang from the church playing "Joy to the World!"

The girl sat down on the steps, rummaged in her backpack.

Suddenly I had to cough.

She looked in my direction. Discovered me. Somehow it was totally embarrassing.

But she nodded to me. Pretty friendly. And I— no idea why—went slowly toward her.

She smiled at me. And I liked her smile.

It was so nice that I sat next to her on the cold steps.

She held out her hand that had thick silver rings on each finger. Her wrists were wrapped with leather bands.

I carefully took her hand.

"I'm Mary. What's your name?"

"Clara!" I said.

She pulled her hand away and said, "Run away?" I nodded. "And you?" I asked.

"I'm on the go!" she said. "Sometimes here, sometimes there!"

"And where are you spending the night?"

She shrugged her shoulders. "I'll see!" she said. The smile was gone. Now she looked sad.

I started to feel the cold. I didn't want to freeze, so I jumped up. "I have to go!" I said.

"Too bad!" she said.

"Come with me!" I said.

This sentence just slipped out of me.

But I thought it was a good thing to say. Totally good. Even though I knew that it was also pretty crazy.

She stared at me. Then she shook her head.

"And why not?"

"Your parents!" she said. "Do you think they will like it if you simply drag me in? And on Christmas Eve?"

"Of course!" I said. "Especially on Christmas Eve!"

"Are you sure?" She looked skeptical.

"Very sure!" I said. "Come, let's go before we freeze!"

And I thought about the story that my father always reads to us on Christmas Eve: No room at the inn . . .

Exactly!

And we have room.

SCENE 4

7:00 p.m. / In front of the house

"Are you sure about this?" Mary looked anxious. Like a little girl.

"Absolutely sure!" I said.

And felt the fear at the nape of my neck. My parents will have a fit. A girl off the street! And especially one who looks like this one . . . just like one imagines! My mother would say "bedraggled!" She would probably throw me out. She wouldn't put up with someone like Mary. And especially not on Christmas Eve.

But I had no choice. I couldn't just leave Mary outside to freeze in the cold.

There were two options. Either my parents would think it was okay. Or they wouldn't.

I rang the doorbell. First once, and then again. My mother ripped the door open. Her face was tear stained. She hugged me.

Then she saw Mary. And the fear was visible in her face.

"Mom! I have a surprise for you!"

SCENE 5
8:00 p.m. / In the living room

It's finally here! Christmas Eve!

Delicious aromas from the kitchen. Lit beeswax candles. The tree with three tops. The Christmas carousel was turning.

My mother set up the music stand. She got her violin. I got my flute.

My father sat at the piano.

And then—like every year—Christmas songs.

Mary had a totally beautiful voice. She should be a singer!

Then my father read the Christmas story . . .

Where it said "and there was no room at the inn" he looked at my mother. By now, she was smiling, completely relaxed.

Then she served the crisp roast goose—well, whatever was left of it.

This year, we only had a partial goose.

And Anton . . .

who probably didn't dare to come in . . .

And yet . . . I just heard something. A cautious meow at the door.

"Let him in, Clara!" said my mother.

She put a juicy potato on Mary's plate. The first one. The second potato was for Dad. This year, I would eat the wings. Because Anton got the tender goose breast.

"Merry Christmas!" said my mother.

She beamed. The stress was lifted and gone. The fits had disappeared.

Totally relaxed, she nibbled the crunchy skin. She smiled at Mary and said: "This is the best Christmas present! That you found our Clara and brought her home. Thank you. A thousand thanks!"

I felt a light kick to my shins. That was Mary's foot. She grinned at me.

I hid my laugh behind my napkin. And I was very happy with this Christmas—more than happy. This was the best I've ever had.

"Thank you, Mary!" I said.

Marjaleena Lembcke
A REAL SANTA CLAUS

As Julia and Tom walked home after the last day of school before Christmas break, they met an old man with a large, shaggy dog. He carried a backpack and held a birch walking stick in his hand. There was snow on his fur hat and icicles in his beard. It was very cold, but he was not wearing any gloves.

Because he was wearing a red, quilted coat, Tom, who was seven years old, grinned and asked the old man, "Are you Santa Claus?"

The dog barked and growled. The man laid his hand on the dog's head. "Quiet," he said to the animal, "quiet!" Then he looked Tom directly in the eyes and asked, "What do you think?" His gaze was sorrowful, and his voice sounded tired. Tom shook his head, embarrassed.

Julia wished the man a Merry Christmas. He did not answer, and the two children continued on.

"Why was he angry?" Tom asked his sister.

"He wasn't angry," answered Julia. "I think he was sad."

"Why was he sad? Because he wants to be Santa Claus?" suggested Tom.

"Because he's homeless."

"What do homeless people do?" asked Tom.

"What do you think they do?"

Julia turned around to look back at the man and his dog. He had stopped and was watching the children. They walked very fast the rest of the way home. Julia did not turn around again.

The next day, Julia and Tom built a big snowman. They gave him eyes of coal, a carrot nose, and put an old twig broom into his hand. By the time the snowman was finished, they almost looked like snowmen themselves. They dusted the snow from their jackets, pants, and mittens. Then they went inside the house to warm up in the kitchen. It was well heated and smelled of fresh baking. Raisin buns and cinnamon rolls were already laid out on the kitchen table. After they hung their mittens to dry on the line above the stove, they sat at the table. Each one picked out their favorite treat.

Tom gave a few crumbs to a starling who sat on the windowsill. Dad had found the bird with a broken wing last fall. He had brought it home and nursed it back to health.

"He'll go back out in the spring," Dad had said. "He can spend the winter with us, while his family is in the south. But as soon as the other starlings return from their travels in the spring, he's going back to his own kind. A starling is not a pet."

The starling pecked at a teaspoon, as if to say, *that spoon belongs to me.* "You aren't a magpie!" said Julia and took the spoon away from him. The bird hopped onto her arm, turned its head to the side, and sang a starling song.

"Can people understand what birds say?" asked Tom.

"Sort of. You can tell whether they are angry, happy, or sad," said Julia.

"Maybe you were wrong. Maybe the homeless person was really angry and not sad," said Tom. "If I see him again, I will ask him."

"Do you want to run after him to ask, 'Excuse me, but are you perhaps angry?'"

"In any case, that dog would have loved to bite us!" said Tom. Then the two forgot about the man and his dog.

There was rustling in the living room. Mother and Father whispered to each other. Now and then, Mother laughed happily.

"They are wrapping the Christmas presents," said Julia.

"But Santa Claus brings the presents," said Tom. He wasn't quite sure if he still believed in Santa, but he always thought it was exciting when there was a knock at the door on Christmas Eve, and the man with the white beard and red coat would appear, set down his sack, and always ask the same question, "What are the names of the children in this house?"

Last year, Tom thought he had recognized his uncle's voice. When his uncle asked about the children's names, he had answered, "But you know them!"

After that, Father thought the time for Santa's visits had come to an end. Santa Claus should go to the younger children. Julia and Tom were already pretty big. When Julia was six, she had found a Santa Claus beard and a red coat in the hall closet. That had been three years ago. Since then, it was hard for her to believe in Santa, even though she liked to read stories about him and thought it was nice that he lived at the North Pole.

It snowed all night, and the pine trees bent under its weight. The driveway to the house was covered with huge snowdrifts. The fields glittered like fine sugar. Father shoveled the driveway and sidewalk. Julia and Tom brushed the new snow off their snowman.

It snowed again the following night.

The next day, on Christmas Eve, Julia and Tom discovered footprints in the snow. They led to and from the snowman. The snowman's nose was missing. The children dug through the snow, but could not find the carrot. They followed the steps, which led to the shed. The prints had been made by someone who wore big shoes.

"Santa Claus!" whispered Tom excitedly.

"I thought you didn't believe in him anymore. And what use does he have for a carrot?" said Julia and she laughed. Then she stopped and held Tom tightly. There were small red spots in the snow.

"Blood!" cried Tom.

Someone had shot a rabbit, thought Julia.

She followed the trail of blood. It passed between the shoe tracks. Julia didn't tell Tom what she was thinking. Many thoughts and questions ran through her head. Had Father shot a rabbit? But why did he take it to the shed? Had Father found a wounded fox and carried it into the shed to bandage it? Father had already saved the lives of many animals.

Julia suddenly remembered the old man and his dog. Maybe those were his tracks. Maybe he had killed his dog. There were no paw prints to be seen. Maybe he was lurking around waiting for them. Maybe he was the one who had stolen the carrot. Maybe he really was a mean old man.

"Maybe Santa Claus hurt himself," said Tom, his voice sounding unsure.

"You know that there's no such thing as Santa Claus!" said Julia.

The tracks stopped in front of the shed. The children listened very carefully. They were scared. From the shed, they heard grumbling.

They turned around on the spot and ran back to the house.

"What's the hurry?" asked Mom, amused, as they tore into the kitchen. "Hungry?"

Simultaneously, Julia and Tom told her about what they had seen and heard.

"A trail of blood and strange voices! Why, this sounds like a murder mystery!" said Father, who put on his jacket and went out to investigate. Julia and Tom sat at the window and watched him. Father went to the shed. As he opened the door, Julia and Tom gripped the windowsill tightly. After a while, Father reappeared at the shed door and closed it behind him. He waved to the children in the window. He returned to the kitchen.

"Was anyone there?" asked Julia.

"Yes," answered Father, "several mice and the wind!"

"What we heard wasn't the sound of mice scurrying!" Tom shook his head.

"But the wind grumbled! He is such a noisy fellow. He always has to see whether he can lift up something or at least scare someone. But, he had little luck with the thick beams in the shed. That's why he grumbled, because the beams didn't shake in fear as he rushed past."

Julia looked at her father doubtfully.

"If anyone is there, he'll have to turn on his flashlight soon. Otherwise, he won't see anything," whispered Tom to his sister.

"If there really is someone there, and if he turns on a flashlight or lights a candle, we'll see the light through the cracks in the shed. But Father wouldn't lie to us," Julia whispered back.

"Only sometimes," said Tom.

Night fell. Julia and Tom watched the shed. They saw neither light nor any movement. Between all of the Christmas preparations, Tom and Julia forgot about the trail of blood, the snowman's nose, and the grumbling in the shed. They washed, put on their best clothes, and went into the kitchen. Mother had already set the table.

"Let's eat quickly and then we can open our presents," Tom said impatiently as he sat down at the table.

Mother and Father looked at each other and smiled.

"You have to wait a little bit. Tonight, we're having company," said Father.

"We never have company on Christmas Eve!" cried Julia.

"This Christmas Eve we will," said Mother.

"Who's coming?" asked Tom.

"Santa Claus," answered Father, smiling. "But before coming in, he has to relax after his long trip."

"There is no Santa Claus," said Julia.

Then, they waited. The candles flickered brightly on the windowsills and cast their small lights into the darkness outside as well.

At the knock on the door, Julia winced. Tom became very pale. Santa Claus entered. He had a gray beard, wore a red coat, carried a backpack on his back, and held his fur hat in his hand. Next to him was a dog, who wagged his tail.

"Merry Christmas!" said the old man.

Julia and Tom returned his greeting a little fearfully. Mother invited the man to sit at the table. The dog got ham and a few bones. The people ate baked ham, carrot casserole, and mashed potatoes. There was blueberry soup with whipped cream for dessert. Then, Dad lit the candles on the Christmas tree. They all gathered in the living room and sang Christmas carols. The old man did not sing along. He merely moved his lips now and then and sighed.

"And now, I'm sure our Santa would like to hand out the presents," said Dad, smiling.

The old man got his backpack. With a somewhat shaky voice, he read the name on each gift. Each time Tom received one, he bowed deeply and said, "Thank you very much, Santa Claus."

And each time Julia picked up a gift for her, she shook the man's hand and whispered, "Thank you."

The old man's cheeks began to glow. The later it got, the more he looked

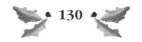

like Santa Claus. Julia thumbed through the book of fairy tales she had gotten. Tom played with his wooden train. And the old man sat at the living room table with Mother and Father in quiet conversation. The old man did not say much. Whenever Julia glanced up from her book, she saw the man looking at her or at Tom. When he looked at Julia, she smiled at him.

Late that night, Mother prepared a mattress in the kitchen for Santa because they did not have a guestroom. The man lay down to sleep, and the dog lay down in front of the mattress. Julia and Tom also went to bed. They slept in the same room. Whispering, they talked about their presents. Mother quietly hummed a Christmas carol. Father checked to see that all of the candles were out.

When all of the lights were off, Santa Claus said, "This was a lovely evening. I thank all of you."

The next morning, the man and his dog were gone. "He could have stayed with us until the spring, until it's warmer," Tom said.

"He could have said good-bye," said Julia.

When they looked at their snowman, they had a surprise. He had a nose again.

"Our Santa stole the carrot!" cried Tom.

"And he also brought it back. Maybe he wanted to eat it, but then he didn't need it anymore because we had ham," suggested Julia.

They followed the fresh footsteps to the shed. But the tracks did not stop there; the trail continued on. It went along the road for as far as their eyes could see.

"Who was that man, really?" Julia asked her father.

"I don't know," Father answered. "When I found him in the shed, his nose was bleeding. I think he hadn't had enough to eat in a long time. I asked him whether he would like to be our guest and whether he would do you the favor of playing Santa Claus. He did that gladly. And then he went his own way again. Perhaps he was Santa."

"In any case, he was the first real Santa Claus we have ever had," said Julia.

Tom nodded.

Father looked out at the white landscape curiously, as if the snow could tell him thousands of stories.

When school started again, Julia and Tom kept an eye out along the roads for an old man with a large shaggy dog. But they never saw him again. In the spring, the starling flew back to the other birds. And in the fall, he traveled to the warm countries with them. In the winter, Julia and Tom built a snowman. No strangers visited him or took away his carrot nose. Only children's footsteps were to be seen around him. In the shed, only the mice scurried and the wind grumbled in the beams.

Christmastime arrived.

On Christmas Eve, Father looked into the shed again. Julia and Tom waited for the knock at the door. Mother repeatedly peered out through the window into the darkness. They waited for a long time before handing out their presents. But Santa Claus did not come. Finally, Julia and Tom gave out the gifts. And it was another nice evening.

Merry Christmas!

First published in the United States, Great Britain, Canada, Australia, and New Zealand in
2006 by North-South Books Inc., an imprint of NordSüd Verlag AG, Gossau Zürich, Switzerland.
Distributed in the United States by North-South Books Inc., New York.

Library of Congress Cataloging-in-Publication Data is available.
A CIP catalogue record for this book is available from The British Library.

ISBN-13: 978-0-7358-2100-2 / ISBN-10: 0-7358-2100-3 (trade edition)
10 9 8 7 6 5 4 3 2 1

Printed in Belgium

**Published in cooperation with Annette Betz Verlag,
a division of Verlag Carl Ueberreuter, Vienna, Austria**